THE STORY OF GREEN RIVER

Also by Holly Webb

THE STORY OF
GREEN RIVER

HOLLY WEBB

Illustrated by ZANNA GOLDHAWK

h HODDER

ORION CHILDREN'S BOOKS

First published in Great Britain in 2022
by Hodder & Stoughton

1 3 5 7 9 10 8 6 4 2

A CIP catalogue record for this book
is available from the British Library.

ISBN 9781 51010 962 9

Printed and bound in Great Britain by Clays Ltd, Elcograf S.p.A.

The paper and board used in this book are made
from wood from responsible sources.

Orion Children's Books
An imprint of
Hachette Children's Group
Part of Hodder & Stoughton Limited
Carmelite House
50 Victoria Embankment
London EC4Y 0DZ

An Hachette UK Company

www.hachette.co.uk
www.hachettechildrens.co.uk

For Jon, Ash, Robin and Will

CHAPTER ONE

The Stronghold

Silken powered up through the water, exploding from the river's surface in a shower of bright droplets and laughing as the sun hit her fur. A burst of tiny rainbows pattered past her nose as the light caught the spray, and Silken twisted like a leaf in the wind before the pull of the river called her back down.

Settling, she floated on her back, her eyes closed against the sun. The water was warm this close to the bank, shallow and calm. She had been working hard enough that she deserved a little rest, she thought, though she peeped sideways to see if any of the other young beavers had noticed her slacking off.

They couldn't even see her here, she realised. They were all further downstream, energetically tackling a fallen tree that was lying half in, half out of the water. With a sigh, Silken turned right side up again, and looked regretfully at the branch she should have been towing. She wasn't sure it was even worth taking it back to the lodge. Frost and Speckle would call it a twig, which was only a bit unfair. It really wasn't very big. She didn't understand how they managed, tossing about great logs the way they did.

'You all right?'

Silken whirled, almost somersaulting round her tail, and the old beaver behind her chuckled. 'Wish my tired bones would let me swirl about like that,' Grizzle said comfortably. 'Fast as a fish you are, girl. What were you doing staring up at the sun?'

'Resting,' Silken said. 'Just for a moment,' she added quickly. She didn't want Grizzle thinking she was smaller and weaker than the others. Silken knew that she was – but she tried not to make it too obvious to everyone else.

It was all very well being as fast as a fish, but that wasn't worth much when it meant her teeth were as weak as a fish's too. For a long time Silken had supposed it was just her age – that her adult teeth would grow in eventually, and then she'd be able to chew through massive tree trunks like the rest of the clan. She was starting to understand that it was never going to happen.

So she busied herself with other jobs. Always there, always helping. Not giving anyone a chance to notice that her teeth could only nibble at tree bark, instead of biting through to the wood beneath.

She *was* good at other things, Silken tried to tell herself, but it was getting harder and harder to listen. Her swimming was fast, acrobatic – but what use were silly tricks? Slow and steady wins the day, her father said. He always seemed to say it just when Silken had swum faster, or dived deeper than the others. To remind her that she had nothing to be proud of.

'Take that piece down to the dam, my little dear,' Grizzle said, nodding downstream. 'I'll go and chase the others. They should have that trunk cleaned up and ready to swim by now.'

Silken nodded. Grizzle hadn't even bothered asking her why she wasn't dressing the tree trunk with Frost and Speckle. She was the useless one, the *little dear*. A funny, undersized creature, willing to help, of course, but not to be counted upon. Silken wondered bitterly how much time the builders spent finding unimportant tasks to keep her busy.

She had been so happy, only moments before. The sunlight on her fur had been such a simple pleasure. Now, she swam on homewards, clumsily guiding the thin branch with her paws, fighting the strong flow of the river as it tried to seize the wood and fling it downstream ahead of her.

She hoped Grizzle wasn't still watching as she squirmed and flailed, hating her weak paws and needle teeth. She was only half in control of the slim branch as the river tumbled her past Frost and Speckle and the others, and she heard Frost's smothered crow of laughter and Speckle hushing him. *Don't care,* she muttered to herself. *Don't care.*

She caught the branch in a strong grip at last, and let the river carry her in towards the bank, and the side channel that led to the dam, and the Great Lodge of Stronghold that was built atop it.

They were in the middle of the springtime rebuilding, securing the dam and the lodge for the year ahead. Silken could see older members of the clan scurrying over the top of the dam, testing the logs, patting in more sealing mud. That was her father up there, Silken realised as she came closer, casting a grim glance over a heavy timber wall from the roof of the lodge. Silken ducked lower in the water, trying to hide behind her branch. She knew she looked bedraggled and exhausted, and she was bringing in a branch her father would give kits to play with.

Her father spotted her, of course, and raised a stiff paw in salute. Russet, one of the junior builders, came darting over to see what Silken had brought in. She was a summer or so older, just recently passed out of her apprenticeship, and quietly proud of herself. She had also obviously been briefed about Master Grey's little daughter. 'Excellent, excellent,' she murmured, smiling cheerfully at Silken. 'I've just the place for that.'

Silken nodded, not wanting any part of that energetic enthusiasm. 'The others are bringing in a big timber any moment now,' she muttered. 'A fallen oak, it looked like, from further upstream. Good and solid.'

Russet brightened for real this time, her whiskers flickering. 'Oh, truly? We need something heavy to brace the main chamber. Definite cracks there, you know.' She glanced eagerly past Silken, hoping to spot the others coming in, and Silken retreated, scurrying out of the corral as she heard them splashing in down the channel.

They were rightly proud. It was a massive tree trunk they'd brought in, one that would have the builders clambering all over it for a day or two, chuckling and muttering to themselves, calling measurements and joyfully tapping at the true heart of the wood. The six young beavers shunted it into the corral, shoving their catch up half on to the bank to ground it good and tight. Silken watched as they dusted off their paws, nudging each other proudly as Russet squeaked at them in delight.

Her own thin branch slipped back into the water, unnoticed. Silken didn't bother to chase after it.

That night she sat between Frost and Speckle, nodding and patting their paws whenever an older clan member came over to praise the tall oak. She was caught up in their celebration without being part of it, and the food was dry and tasteless in her mouth.

'Here, try this.' Frost passed her a clay dish of delicately braised reed hearts, a treat that the cook had set before them with a laugh and a ruffle of Frost's silver-tipped fur. That kind of special dish was usually kept for the most senior builders. Everyone, all through the lodge, had heard about the young ones' mighty catch.

'No!' Silken pushed it away, slopping the herb sauce over the side.

'Hey!' Frost peered at her in the candlelight. 'What's up with you?'

'Nothing.' Silken stared down at her plate. She tried to swallow another mouthful of pickled marsh marigold, but it caught in her throat, leaving her spluttering. Frost thumped her hard on the back, nearly sending Silken face-first into her dinner.

'Sorry!' Frost boomed cheerfully, yanking her back on to the bench. 'Don't know my own strength sometimes.'

Silken longed to hit him back, or deal him a savage bite in the soft fur below his throat, or fling that dish of waterlogged reed hearts in his face. But she wouldn't. Her father was watching, for a start. Besides, Frost hadn't done anything wrong. He'd done everything right. That was what was so hard.

'Silken, won't you sing for us?' Speckle laid a dappled paw over hers. 'One of those story songs you tell about the grey beaver and his travels. Can we have the one where he goes all the way downstream and finds the sea?'

'Not now,' Silken said. 'No one wants a song – they want to talk to you about that tree.'

I don't want to sing, was what she really meant. None of the others sang, although a few of the younger beavers would thump the tables to keep a rhythm for her or stamp their feet. Singing was another thing that made Silken strange. She had begun to chant and chatter to herself as just a little thing, or so they told her, making up sweet strings of nonsense about the ripples and the waves and the singing wind in the rushes. She'd only sung to amuse the other kits at first, but a few times now the younger ones had pushed her up at dinner and made her sing for the whole company.

'Make a song about our tree!' Frost yelled excitedly, and he and Speckle each grabbed her by a paw and lifted her up on to the table among the plates and dishes. Silken couldn't see a way to get down without singing. She stared down at the timbers of the table for a moment, catching up her tail in her paws and kneading at it. She didn't see the troubled eyes of a few of the older clan, as they watched her stroke her tail tip thoughtfully under her chin. No other beaver would do *that*, not ever.

At last Silken began to hum a low quiet note, a strange sound that cut through the chatter in the hall, and made the beavers lay down their last morsels of candied daisy or nut cake, to watch the youngling standing on the table.

She sang.

> *I stood tall, above the rushes,*
> *My branches clawing to the sky.*
> *Tall I stood all your clan's lifetime,*
> *But in your hearts, you heard me sigh.*

It was a strange and mournful song, and Silken heard the whispers round the tables. An uncertain muttering, a shifting of paws.

'This isn't what I meant at all,' Frost growled to Speckle, loud enough for Silken to hear. 'I meant about how we brought it in, not this airy-fairy sort of stuff.'

But Speckle only shoved him sideways and went on

listening. Silence fell gradually over the rest of the company too, their talk of woodwork and foraging dying away to nothing. The beavers listened, and the song twined itself inside them, and set down roots.

Silken did not feel as though she chose to stop singing – the song simply ended. She stood blinking uncertainly atop the table, lost for a moment.

'Here.' Speckle was in front of her, holding out a paw to help her down, and Silken scrambled gratefully off the table, anxious to hide herself away from all the watching eyes. There seemed to be hundreds, gleaming at her in the candlelight.

'What was all that about?' Frost whispered to her when she was back on the bench. Silken stared back at him dazedly. 'I thought you were going to sing about how clever we were to bring in such a great tree,' he added grumpily. 'Not gloomy stuff about roots and sap and dying.'

'I'm sorry. It was just what came to me,' Silken murmured, trying to catch the wisps of words inside her head. She peered around the hall, noting that the company was oddly silent now. From the sidelong glances she kept intercepting, the song had something to do with it.

Silken sighed. There was nothing she could do about it. She grabbed a piece of nut cake, suddenly starving, and sat hunched and nibbling, trying not to listen to the conversation floating around the hall.

'She's such an odd little thing, isn't she? That eerie song, wherever did she learn something like that!'

'Poor Master Grey.'

'Well, these things do happen, when you . . .' The speaker's eyes bulged a little as a companion stuck a sharp elbow in his side. He shot a glance across at Silken and subsided.

Silken sank her shoulders lower, and made a show of eating the nut cake, though the sweetness was gluing her teeth together, and it left her feeling sick.

She was just wondering how soon she could slip away without anyone noticing when she heard a rustling and a whispering and glanced around to see that her father was approaching.

The beavers believed that each and every creature in the clan was equal, so they had no such thing as a high table; but as the Master Builder, her father sat at what would have been the high table if they had one. Silken and her companions were far down the other end of the hall, and every beaver that Master Grey passed on his journey through the room made sure to nod at him and murmur their evening wishes.

'It's late, small one,' Grey said to her, his voice a low rumble that carried round the tables. Silken hurriedly slid down from the bench and followed him, wishing that he would call her by her name. He seemed to make a point of reminding everyone that his only child was small and strange. Still, she wanted to go.

Silken scurried after him down the hall, and through the maze of passages to their sleeping quarters, two interconnected rooms off a small gathering place.

'That song,' her father said, his voice so quiet that Silken had to lean close to hear. 'Where did it come from?'

She blinked at him uncomfortably. He didn't like her to draw attention to herself, and he didn't approve of her singing. He had never forbidden her to do it, but she knew it worried him. In truth, Silken thought dismally as her father hung up the lantern on the wall, he did not want *this* daughter noticed for anything. It was a very short step to thinking that he did not want her at all.

'I don't know,' she whispered. 'I didn't make it up. At least, I don't think I did.' She bowed her head, waiting for him to tell her that was nonsense, and wondering if she should have lied. But the strength of the words and those long sad notes was still somewhere inside her, and she could not deny them.

Her father nodded, as though he'd expected something of the kind. 'Be careful, small one,' he muttered, and this time she didn't mind the pet name as much. His concern for her was there in the growling of his voice, and the clumsiness of his massive old paws as he bunched up the small reeds to make her a soft bed.

'Is it wrong, to sing?' she asked hesitantly.

'It's different.' He turned to look at her. 'Different is . . . not wrong, but it can be dangerous.' He sighed. 'I don't know what to do with you, little one,' he went on, almost to himself. 'Perhaps we should go upriver and ask the swan. He might have some advice, if we can find him. If he'll talk.'

Silken hung her head. She was so much trouble. It was hard to hear her father – her father who was so strong! – admit that he needed help, that he didn't understand her, didn't know what to do with her. And why would the old swan know better than her own father?

Silken had met the swan once before as a tiny kit, scurrying through the reeds after her father. The huge bird had been daunting, his neck long and snake-like, his speech a curious mixture of hisses and barks that she'd found hard to understand. The thought of talking to that strange creature made her feel cold inside.

'I'll try harder,' she said.

Her father didn't answer her, but she knew that it was what he had been wanting to hear. His paws were still clumsy as he reached out to stroke the top of her head. He had never found it easy to show affection – never seized her in his arms or swung her around as other fathers did.

As a younger child she had wished that he would hug her, but she'd grown used to how he was. Now, that clumsy touch made her want to hang on to his paw and not let go. But she was too old to crawl into his lap these days, even if she was still small enough.

Perhaps if my mother were still alive, things would be easier, she thought, for the hundredth time. Silken had been so young when her mother had died that she didn't remember her at all. It seemed to hurt her father when she begged for stories, so she had stopped asking long ago.

Her father turned away from her, padding into his own room. Through the opening between the two she saw him wrap his paw around a small wooden box that was pushed to the back of a shelf. He glanced back at Silken, and she knew that he was waiting for her to be safely in her bed, so that he could open it.

Inside, she knew, was a green scarf, finely woven out of rush fibres and dyed with some sort of bright leaf. On other nights, when he thought she was already sleeping, she had crept to the door and seen him take the scarf out and wrap his paws in it. He fell asleep that way sometimes, his head pillowed on the shining fabric.

'Goodnight,' she whispered now. She curled up into the sweet grass bed, and sighed. *Maybe tomorrow*, she thought, as she had so many times before.

Maybe tomorrow I'll be bigger. Maybe tomorrow I'll be like the others. Maybe tomorrow he'll be proud of me.

CHAPTER TWO

The Stronghold

Silken's work detail for the next few days was to help with the final dressing and placing of the great timber that Frost and Speckle and the others had brought in. Her father wanted her there with the others, she realised, even if she wasn't much use. He wanted her not to be different.

The timber was to be placed at the back of the lodge to brace the existing wall, which had been part of the original build and was weakened by age. The timbers that supported the ceiling had shifted, and now the inner wall was showing cracks, dark streaks that split the swirling patterns of coloured clay in the main chamber.

Silken's thin little paws were actually useful for digging out the old anchor mud around the original timber, and she scurried about, burrowing neatly underneath the log while the others chewed through the width of the timber – a job that was far easier than it should have been. The wood was crumbling to dust in their jaws.

'No wonder the wall's cracking,' Frost said, frowning at it.

Even Silken had to admit that the new oak trunk was worth all the fuss and praise. She might not be able to work with wood the way the others did, but she'd had the same training, and she could see the sweet strength of the tree. It whispered to her whenever she touched it, still singing its story. She kept having to pull herself away, before someone caught her daydreaming again.

As the others dragged and shoved the new timber up to take the place of the old, one of the builders sent Silken downstream to fetch more clay to seal the great trunk in. She darted away to the muddy bank, feverishly digging and dumping pawfuls of clay mud into the reed basket. She had to be there when the trunk was finally settled. It was a moment that would be remembered, and too many of the clan would notice if she wasn't there – her father would see them notice.

When the reed basket was full enough at last, Silken strapped it around her shoulders and darted out into the water, swimming for the lodge to join Speckle and Frost.

'There you are!' Frost was perched atop the new trunk now, bright-eyed with pride. Speckle and some of the other young ones were at the other end, watched beadily by one of the builders.

'Pass me that basket, Silken,' Frost called down. 'We need more clay to get it properly fast.'

A small crowd of beavers was gathering around the bottom of the wall, watching as the huge timber was settled into place. The younger kits had wormed their way through to the front and were gazing up at Frost. They all adored him, and he was so gentle, even though he was big. Often, he'd let the small ones climb all over him, and sometimes he would even swim out into the great river with them perched on his back, splashing wildly and squeaking with excitement.

Silken stretched up, handing her basket to Frost, and he leaned down to snatch it from her. She wasn't sure what exactly happened – even after, when she tried to think it through, she couldn't slow it down enough to see. Was it Frost's weight that had set the timber sliding? Or had one of the props slipped?

It made no difference. All that mattered was the soft creak, and the tremor running through the great tree trunk. Silken saw Frost's face wrinkle. His paws skittered on the bark as the timber shifted, and Silken screamed, 'Jump!'

Frost flung himself off the tree trunk as it began to fall. He leaped out into the knot of watchers, since there was nowhere else to go, and they scattered. There was a chorus of splashes as they dived into the water, and then turned to look back in horror at the oak tree's splintering, tearing fall, and at the cracks that raced outward along the wall above the hole.

It was a disaster. All that effort, and now the lodge was in a worse state than ever. Silken peered up between a mess of sticks at the edge of the lodge and flattened her ears in distress. So much work, wasted.

Someone whined.

Silken looked down from the cracked wall, her heart suddenly in her throat. The massive tree trunk was resting on the mud path around the lodge now, at a sickening, broken angle. And pressed tight against the wall behind it was the littlest beaver kit, frozen with fear. He had run the wrong way in a panic, Silken guessed, or tried to escape the stumbling crowd by pressing up against the wall.

'Brindle!' A frantic howl arose, and Silken and the other beavers turned to see Tawny, the kit's mother, surging through the water. The kit whined again, wriggling behind the massive trunk.

'Keep still,' Silken called to him, and Speckle stretched out her paws, murmuring, 'Brindle, don't move, in case it shifts again . . .'

The kit froze, staring at them with wide, terrified eyes.

'Silken, get back.' Frost leaped up on to the path. He

braced the trunk with his shoulder, and reached a long paw underneath to haul out the trembling kit.

His mother seized him, frantically patting and parting his fur. 'Are you hurt? What happened? How did you get under there?' she gabbled. The kit was too breathless and scared to reply; he just cuddled in against her, eyes tight shut.

'This is your fault!'

Silken recoiled as the mother turned on her, teeth bared, eyes glittering with fright – and malice.

'No – I—' she started to protest, but Tawny kept coming, hissing and cursing, the baby still clutched against her.

'You did this, of course it was you!' Tawny's voice rose to a shriek, and Silken stood frozen, letting the stream of fury pour over her. She didn't dare move. *Had* she hurt Brindle?

Tawny swiped at her viciously, and instinct made Silken duck out of the way at last – just not fast enough. Curved black claws raked along the side of her muzzle. Silken stumbled back, almost falling against Frost, pressing her paws against the scratch.

'Hey! What are you going after Silken for? She didn't do anything,' her friend protested, steadying her with one huge paw. 'I was the one up on the tree, I must have let it slip somehow. All Silken did was hand me the basket. If you're going to take your claws to someone, it should be me!'

'Don't you try and protect her!' Tawny snarled at him. 'It was her, it must have been. She doesn't belong here! Get out, you! Get out!' Frost drew in a surprised huff of breath and drew back a little, pulling Silken and Speckle with him. Tawny was smaller than he was, but anger had made her vicious.

'It was an accident.' The shadow of a larger beaver fell across them, and Tawny drew back, looking uncertain in the presence of the Master Builder.

'You would say that.' Tawny was quieter now, and she darted a nervous glance at Silken's scratched muzzle. But then she added sharply, 'Of course you would, since you call her your daughter.'

Silken saw her father's face darken. Was he blaming her too? She knew that, as his daughter, everything she did reflected back on him. *Had* she caused the tree to fall? She would never do something like that on purpose – but what if she'd been distracted, her head still half full of song? She had been right next to the tree, after all, her paws almost touching it, and it did keep on singing to her. Perhaps she hadn't realised what she was doing.

'I didn't mean to,' she whispered shakily to her father and Frost, one paw still held over the oozing scratch. 'I didn't . . .'

'You didn't do *anything*,' Frost growled. 'You weren't even touching the tree. Like I said, if it was anyone it was me.

21

And she should have been taking better care of her kit!' he added, glaring at Tawny.

'Look at Silken,' Speckle put in, lightly touching Master Grey's paw. 'Tawny scratched her.'

Silken looked up at her father, wishing that it was him speaking for her instead of her friends. Didn't *he* care that Tawny had drawn blood, that she was still bleeding?

'The tree falling was an accident,' Silken's father said again, his voice calm and low. It hummed, silencing the chatter of the other beavers, all now climbing up out of the water, and surging around the fallen timber. 'Ill fortune, that's all – the old wolf passed us too close.'

The crowd watching shivered and muttered, flicking their paws to shake away the bad luck.

'Stay back, dam-builders, it may slip again.' Master Grey eyed the wreckage and sighed. 'We will need to assess the wall, to see if it needs shoring up before we raise the timber.' He looked around sternly, and the growing chorus of whispers died away. 'We *must* try again. The wall needs repairing, no foolish superstition changes that.'

Then he moved slowly towards Tawny, pushing Silken gently in front of him. 'Is your kit injured?' he asked, and though his voice was kind, Silken felt a strange shiver run along the roots of her fur. There was an undertone to her father's words, something she had never heard in his voice before. Something that sounded like fear.

'No,' Tawny said. 'No thanks to her.'

Silken flinched, but her father merely nodded.

'Good. Perhaps you should take him inside anyway. Drink a soothing tea, both of you.'

'Trying to get rid of me,' Tawny muttered, but she hurried away, and Silken saw several other beavers join her, all mothers of the young kits who had been crowded around. They were going to gossip, she realised miserably. Whatever her father and Frost said about it being an accident, they knew who they wanted to blame.

'Show me the cut.' Silken's father rubbed his paw gently down her jawline, and she ducked her head. 'A scratch. You weren't hurt when the tree fell?'

'No. I got out of the way,' she said, wishing that he'd hold her.

'And you, Frost?'

'Twisted a paw leaping down to the path, that's all.'

Silken's father looked round at Speckle huddled close at the edge of the path, and she shook her head. 'I'm not hurt,' she murmured. 'Only – only surprised.'

'What did we do wrong?' Frost asked, gazing at the tree.

'You did nothing wrong, Frost. Who knows why it fell.'

Silken's father sighed. 'Bad luck, like I said. The tree is still strong. We will raise it again.'

'Won't everyone . . .' Silken hesitated. She knew that everyone would talk. They'd say the timber was cursed – that the old wolf had breathed on it now. They'd want to lever it over the dam and let it float away down the channel to the river, let the wolf and the water have it.

Her father gazed at her silently, and Silken looked away. She didn't want to meet his eyes. Even though he seemed to be sure the falling tree was an accident, Silken still felt guilty.

'Should we start to raise the tree again?' the young builder Russet asked, approaching Silken's father respectfully.

He looked around, noting the silent gathering of builders, the anxious eyes. 'I wish I could tell you all to rest,' he said, raising his voice. 'But the wall has cracked, my friends. We can't risk leaving it any longer, in case the damage worsens. Take a breath. We start again.'

The younger beavers scurried off to take their places. Silken went after them, still feeling sick inside, but her father called her back.

'Perhaps you should rest, small one. You're shocked still. And that encounter with Tawny – you're hurt. She frightened you.'

Silken shook her head. She didn't want to be sent away! The others were carrying on, and Frost had been the one who hurt himself, not her. The scratch on her muzzle was only shallow. 'I can help,' she said quickly. 'I'm all right.'

'You should lie down, Silken,' Frost called back to her, and she saw Speckle nodding. 'Rest a bit.'

'But I don't need to!' Silken said again, her voice cracking. 'Please!'

Her father had already turned away. Silken couldn't tell if he'd not heard her pleading, or he was choosing not to listen.

Did they all blame her then, even though they said out loud that it was an accident, just the old wolf looking them over? Silken crept along the path, wondering where she should go. Not back inside the lodge – to reach her room she'd have to pass Tawny and all those gossiping mothers, hissing spite. They'd be silent as she hurried past, but then she'd hear the whispers again behind her, sharp as claws.

Instead, she dived off the path, over the fierce rampart of sticks and thorns, into the pool below the dam. She sank down to the bottom of the channel with scarcely a splash, feeling the dark water welcome her in. It was so quiet down here. The faint murmur of the air bubbles rising out of her fur. A swish – more felt than heard – of a great fish passing by somewhere above. So cold, so peaceful.

She could stay here. Silken shuddered at the thought. What if she did? She could stay in the water – not for ever, of course, she'd have to come up to the surface to breathe, and she'd have to leave the river to groom and waterproof her fur every so often. But she didn't have to go back to the lodge.

She could swim out to the great river and travel on instead. The thought was exciting and horrifying all at the same time. She could just keep on going for ever – or perhaps until she found somewhere she did belong, where she didn't get all those sidelong looks, and whispered comments. Where she wasn't the only one who sang.

Silken wasn't sure that such a place really existed, but right now, she felt as if anywhere would be better than here. She had tried to pretend to herself for such a long time, but pretending wasn't working any more. She was miserable, and home didn't feel like home.

They'd be safer without you, the water whispered, *and happier too.*

CHAPTER THREE

The Holt, upriver from the Stronghold

Sedge surfaced, shaking the water out of his whiskers, and scrambled up on to the bank. There was a thick mat of flattened reeds he remembered here, hidden, but warm in the sunshine. He peered cautiously around the tall stems, and then leaped on to the reed couch, rolling luxuriously to squeeze the water out of his fur. Then he curled up in the sun, and started to lick his coat back into shape.

The river was high again. Too high. He could hear the soft lapping of the water close up against his nest, and in late spring, the reed mat should be high and dry. He had spent weeks learning the river levels by rote, and they had stuck.

He was probably missing another lesson right now. Sedge chuckled softly to himself. Teasel would be searching for him. He should be learning his eddies and currents, or migration patterns, or star reading. Instead he was sunning himself on a pile of reeds, and no one knew where he was.

Teasel might haul him before his mother when he eventually sneaked back, but he didn't care. Or just now he didn't. Sedge rolled over, turning his pale underside to the warm sun, and closed his eyes, letting the heat seep through his fur and banish the chill of the water. Greenriver flowed snow-laden from the mountains, and the waters were shaded by trees for much of their course. Even this late in spring, the river was cold. His breath whistled, and his paws sagged gently on to his front.

A fly whined close by Sedge's nose, and he flipped a paw at it sleepily, trying to get back to his gentle doze. But it was no good – he was awake again, and the guilt was nibbling at him, chasing away the sunlit sleepiness. He twisted upright with a wheezy little groan, and sloped reluctantly back through the reeds to the edge of the river, sliding down the muddy bank. Sedge slipped into the cold green water with hardly a splash. On the surface, a few bright bubbles popped, and then the young otter was gone.

He surfaced a little way up the river, only his eyes and nose showing. He wasn't far from the holt, and he didn't want to be seen, not yet. If he could sneak back inside without being spotted, he could claim that he had been helping out in the storerooms all the time, or visiting the elderly otters gossiping and dozing on the sandbank.

He wouldn't want to *lie*, exactly. But he could let Teasel think he'd been at his heir's duties, couldn't he? No one needed to know that he'd slipped away. All he wanted was a little time to himself, without the watching eyes and the whispers, and the sense that everyone, everywhere, was measuring him up and finding him wanting.

He brushed a paw across his whiskers, checking for scraps of crayfish shell. The heir should never have dirty whiskers. Sedge paddled closer to home, keeping out in the middle of the stream as he approached the huge old willow tree that sheltered the Greenriver holt. The tree leaned right out over the water, and the branches were weighted with golden catkins, dabbling on the surface. Sedge wove his way between them, watching cautiously for the sentries. They'd be perched on the tree roots, stone knives half drawn, ready to race along the bank, or dive into the water at the first sign of an intruder. He'd never get all the way into the holt without one of them spotting him, but if he could creep up under the roots, he could pretend he'd just popped out of a side door. They wouldn't know.

He was so intent on the guards – one heavy old dog otter who looked half asleep, and one dark-furred she otter, gazing downstream towards him with narrowed eyes – that he didn't see the shadow closing in beside him. Then thick blunt whiskers tickled his muzzle, and he turned head over heels in the water with surprise. Teasel spoke in his ear.

'Where have you been then?'

'Nowhere! I mean, here! I'm here! That's where I've been, I've been here!' Sedge spluttered. It felt like he'd swallowed half the river.

'Dear, dear.' Teasel trod water, eyeing him thoughtfully. 'You seem very worried, for a little otter who's been *here* all this time.' Teasel pressed her grizzled old muzzle close to Sedge's. 'What were you doing here *exactly*?'

'Swimming . . .?' Sedge tried, hopefully.

'Oh, swimming.' Teasel nodded. Then she darted in, snapping her sharp teeth a whisker's width in front of Sedge's muzzle and snarled, 'And what were you *supposed* to be doing, Sedge Greenriver?'

Sedge stared back at her, round-eyed and feeling guilty again. It was the *Greenriver* that did it. He and his mother were the only otters so named – it was an honour to carry the name of the holt. But lately, he was only ever Greenriver when he'd done something wrong. Or let someone down. Let *himself* down, that was what Teasel would say, but Sedge knew it was his mother who'd be disappointed. Again.

'Learning bird calls,' he muttered, sinking low in the water, so that only his eyes and ears showed.

'*Vital* bird alarm calls, so you can help guard your holt,' Teasel said. 'What was more important than that, little lord pup?'

'Nothing,' Sedge growled sulkily. The guilt was beginning to fade, turning to anger. Teasel had caught him, hadn't she? Did she have to go on and on?

Teasel hissed. '*Nothing.* Not even an excuse.'

'You'd never believe me anyway!' Sedge eyed the older otter resentfully. He'd only been away a little while. Couldn't he have some time splashing in the sun? All the others got to play. He could hear them now, wrestling with each other in the shallows under the roots.

'Go on,' Sedge muttered, as Teasel paddled to the bank and hustled him out of the water. 'You might as well say it.' He scratched at the biscuity mud with his front claws so he didn't have to look up. He knew Teasel's curled lip and sagging ears quite well enough.

'Say what?' Teasel rumbled curiously, and Sedge muttered an answer. He didn't need to say it aloud – Teasel knew what he meant. He flinched as the old she otter tucked a paw under his chin, and made him look up.

'That I'll never be good enough!' Sedge snarled, snapping at Teasel's claws.

'Mind out, youngster, no biting,' the old otter growled. 'Is that what you think?' she added, leaning down to look close into Sedge's eyes.

Sedge wriggled uncomfortably. 'I suppose. I mean, it's what everybody else thinks. Mother said it.'

'Your mother?' Teasel snorted. 'I doubt that, little lordling. She thinks the sun shines out of your spraints.'

'I heard her talking, a few weeks back,' Sedge whispered, his voice only just above a breath. 'Talking to you! She said I wasn't like my father.'

Teasel gave a hooting sort of laugh. 'Too right!' she spluttered, and Sedge shrank down further into the mud.

His father was a traveller, an adventurer. The sort of otter who had songs written about him. The Greenriver otters loved to sing of the time he'd been grievously injured defending them against an attack from a warlike holt that lived further up the river. He was a hero.

Of course Sedge knew he wasn't anything like his father, and yet it still hurt to hear Teasel say it to his face. But then the old otter patted Sedge's muzzle affectionately. 'Your father, may the waters carry him ever onward, is a giant, little lord pup. Twice the size of me. Tail like a tree branch.'

Sedge peered up at her. 'That's all she meant? That I'm not very big?' He thought for a moment. 'I'm not *that* small, am I?' he asked anxiously. He knew he was slender, compared to some of the other pups.

'You'll grow.' Teasel nodded. 'But perhaps never as big as Campion, or as pale. He's like a great grey ghost. That's all your mother meant.'

'Oh.' Sedge mulled this over silently for a moment, until Teasel nudged him, sending him sideways.

'Eavesdroppers never hear good of themselves, little lord pup.'

'I suppose,' Sedge agreed, feeling foolish. Had he really woven this all out of one misunderstood remark? He shuffled his paws in the mud again. 'But . . . I'm not very clever either. I mean, I take ages to learn everything you're teaching me, and I'm not a strong swimmer, not like the others.'

'You're doing all right,' Teasel told him gruffly.

'I remembered the water levels.' Sedge brightened a little, wriggling so that his fur stood up in sharp brown points. 'The river's high, isn't it? Higher than it should be.' He looked hopefully at the older otter, and then faltered. Teasel was gazing back at him, her expression bleak. 'We learned about the river levels at the quarter moon.' Teasel said nothing and Sedge sagged down again. 'Maybe I got it wrong.'

Teasel licked his ear gently, and Sedge twitched in surprise.

'You know you're right, little lord pup,' Teasel rumbled in his ear. 'Stand up and say so.'

'But you looked angry.'

'Not angry. *Worried.* You're right, the river levels are higher than they should be. Dangerous high. Never seen them like this.' Teasel coiled herself around the younger otter, and nuzzled at him. 'See. You aren't so slow.'

Sedge brightened. It was about the nicest thing the grumpy old otter had ever said to him. But then he peered up. 'Dangerous?' he repeated, his muzzle wrinkling. 'How?'

'There's water in the lower store caverns already. That's why your mother had them all cleared out a few days back. And it's still rising.' Teasel shivered. 'One night of heavy rain and the river could flood.'

Sedge swallowed.

A flood.

The word shouldn't send him shivering home to the holt and his mother. He was a water creature, after all. The river fed him and housed him and lulled him to sleep. A flood was only more water.

But the river was twitchy, temperamental. Treacherous, even – now more than she ever had been. And so very powerful. She chuckled along, pattering over the stones, boiling darkly in the pools and falls, never the same two days running. Half the lore Sedge had learned from his tutor was about reading the river, interpreting her little ways.

'How much of a flood?' he asked huskily.

Teasel shrugged. 'Who knows? It was over our paws down in the storerooms this morning.' She squinted up at the sky. 'Clouds are gathering in the west already. Could be a storm coming – or then again, it could blow over, just as easily. A few days of sun and the store caverns could be dry earth again.' She sighed, and then patted one of the younger otter's paws. 'Whatever happens, I doubt we're heading for a Dark Spring, Sedge. Not so soon after last year. Don't worry.' Then she let out a growling sort of snort. 'Mind you, two of the sentries didn't turn up for their duties this morning.'

Sedge's eyes widened. Had the night wolf passed along the riverbank, and gobbled the missing sentries down? Not that he believed in the night wolf, or not exactly.

Then he realised what Teasel meant. 'They *left*?' he squeaked.

'Uh-huh. Sneaked off by moonlight, the cowards. Not even the grace to say goodbye. Heading for somewhere safer. Fools. No otter should journey alone, not in times like these.'

'Do you think the holt's really in danger?' Sedge asked, watching Teasel stare out at the water. He was trying to look calm and like the lady's heir – not a frightened little pup. But if otters were leaving! It was too difficult to understand. The holt wasn't just where otters lived. They *were* Greenriver otters. It was their belonging.

No one would give that up – or he had never thought so.

'*Could* a Dark Spring come again so soon?' he asked, his voice catching.

Teasel only hunched up her shoulder, still gazing out across the river.

The Dark Spring wasn't often mentioned around the otter pups. If a knot of older otters were talking together but they hushed as soon as the young ones came close, those were the two words left settling in the silence.

A holt was comfortable, cosy even, especially on a winter's night. But it could never be entirely safe. Otters lived half in, half out of the water. That was their way and they couldn't do anything else. It left them vulnerable when the river turned – because the Greenriver loved her otters, until she didn't.

Stories of floods went far back in the history of the holt, times when the river changed, surging up in a cruel flash that broke and battered the holt and the riverbank. Floods had always happened – but usually only once in a generation. Lately though, the waters had come creeping close to the holt every spring.

As the lady of the holt, Sedge's mother spent half her days watching the water, looking for the signs written up in the old books. The holt's lady – or lord, as it might be – was the messenger between the otters and the river. However much love and ceremony the otters poured out on the water, the river was always hard to predict, and sometimes she could be cruel.

Last spring, Sedge's first, the river had risen very suddenly, a storm surge sweeping down from the mountains overnight and flooding the holt entirely. Sedge had been washed out of his cosy bedchamber, tumbling over and over in the rushing water. Otter babies aren't born able to swim, and Sedge was too young and tiny to have learned. He was helpless.

His mother and the other otters swam after him, chasing desperately out to search among the driftwood and weeds washing about in the flood. They found him in the deepest heart of the river and tore him back out of Lady River's clutches, half drowned.

And now the seasons had turned, and it was spring again.

'Why is the river so high?' Sedge asked.

'Wish we knew.' Teasel heaved a massive sigh that shook Sedge's whiskers. 'Something going on upstream, your lady mother reckons. But it's more likely just been a wet season. Seem to have been a lot of those recently. Your mother's holding a ritual tonight, to talk sweetly to the river.' Teasel squinted along the bank towards the holt, and then looked up at the position of the sun. 'We haven't got long. You need to be getting ready. Best sash. Ceremonial dagger. A new wreath.'

Sedge groaned.

Teasel snorted. 'Very fetching you'll look too. The other cubs have been weaving them all afternoon, while you were off truanting.' She scrubbed the fur on top of Sedge's head with her claws. 'You can tell your lady mother that we were out looking at the river levels. It's important for a future lord of the holt to understand the threat of rising water. And you did notice it, at least, without me even prompting you. Now, mind you conduct yourself properly at this ceremony. Everyone will be watching, and they'll all have half an eye on you, little lord pup. Better get going.'

Teasel trundled up to the top of the bank, following the faint path through the long grass and nettles. To an outsider, it would seem no more than a hollow between the stems, a patch of flattened grass here and there, but to the otters it was a path as clear as day.

Sedge darted after her, trying to comb his scattered thoughts into place. He had been dwelling on his mother's words for days, and now it turned out that was all for nothing. He felt as if a sudden eddy had swirled him round and dropped him over a waterfall. He was upside down and inside out. He should have asked her.

Sedge let out a tiny sigh. It wasn't that easy, though, to talk to his mother. She was always busy, for a start. The lady of the holt's duties never ended. Even at meals she was on show, sharing the best dishes with an otter who had served the holt well, or soothing down some worry or quarrel. Sedge would watch and wonder beside her. His mother knew everything. She remembered everything.

When she did have time to talk to him, it was always about serious things – water levels or the old lore, or where medicines were stored in the lower cavern storerooms. Things that the heir to the holt needed to know, things that Sedge struggled to remember. Wasn't all that enough for him to worry about? He didn't want to know that the river was flooding too. He didn't want to hear about the creatures forced out of their homes and lairs by the rising water. Creatures who came creeping downstream to lurk around the Greenriver holt.

Sedge felt his fur rise up as the great willow tree that held the otter holt came into sight.

He didn't remember the last Dark Spring.

He didn't *let* himself remember. Not when he was awake, anyway. He couldn't stop himself dreaming.

⋙⁘⁙⫘⫘⫘⫘⫘

'Sedge!' Lady Thorn wrapped a paw around his head and kissed him, ignoring Sedge trying to pull away. 'I haven't seen you all day.' She held him at arm's length and sighed. 'You need to tidy yourself up, little one, you're muddy. Go on back to your room, you haven't long before we begin.'

Sedge nodded. He'd already noted that his mother had shining river-quartz and seed-pearls set into her claws and strung about her neck. An embroidered belt carried her stone dagger, and a great crown of reeds sat proudly above her deep-set black eyes. It almost hid the shadows and strain creasing her furred muzzle.

'Hurry now,' his mother called, shooing him towards their quarters. 'We can't start without you, dearest.'

Sedge clumped through the main hall of the holt and up the smoothed earth ramp to the upper gallery, where his mother and the elders of the holt now had their quarters. There were larger chambers down below, and the lords and ladies of the holt had always been quartered there, but the great flood last spring had changed all that. Now everyone wanted the higher, safer rooms among the tree roots, and even up into the hollow trunk.

His own room was a little side chamber next to his mother's, only just large enough for a soft bed of fresh-cut reeds, strewn with a couple of blankets. Sedge squinted, trying to see by the lantern hanging from the wall out on the gallery. He licked and dabbed at his coat, combing muddy fragments from his pale belly fur, and scraping his claws on a fat river pebble.

His own flower crown was waiting on the carved wooden shelf above his bed, and he lifted it up with a disgusted sniff. Willow wands and little purple saxifrages – and even a tiny yellow waterlily in the middle. Someone was trying to make him look like a real fishbrain. He considered biting the lily off, but whoever had woven the crown was bound to notice and say something. He jammed the wreath on, wriggling his ears to make it fit – with the waterlily firmly at the back.

Then he dashed back out to the gallery, walking upright to keep his claws clean.

The hall was busy now, full of otters fussing with flowers and smoothing each other's fur. The crowd parted for Sedge as he came down the ramp, and he ducked his head, embarrassed.

'Stand up straight,' Teasel growled behind him, and then she added, 'Nice waterlily there.'

Sedge turned round to glare at her, but he did try to straighten his back, resting one paw on the slim flint dagger in his belt. There were approving mutters all around him, though he did spot a couple of the pups his own age sniggering at the stupid wreath. Sedge glared back, and mouthed, 'Just you wait,' at Lily and Tormentil. Then he marched out to the front of the holt and came to stand by his mother on the roots of the old willow tree.

They were waiting for the sun to be caught in the branches of the willow before they could start the singing. It was sinking very slowly, fiery white in the deep blue of the sky. The breeze was snapping the willow branches, and there was a tide of whispers and shushing and whispers again as the crowd shifted and stared at the sky.

The garland itched.

'Nearly there,' Thorn murmured.

'Now!' his mother cried, and all the holt began to sing, praising the springtime and the river and the trees, their voices swelling and rising to a wild chorus. Sedge could feel the love and fear entwined together in the singing as he caught paws with his mother on one side and a grey-muzzled otter who was one of the sentry guard on the other. All the petty squabbles over kitchen duties and fishing rotas and cleaning were left behind as the otters' voices swelled, even the smallest cubs chirruping in time.

The song died away, and Sedge's mother stepped forward. One of her attendants handed her a polished river mussel shell, the pearly insides glowing pink in the evening sun. Thorn leaned down to scoop up water with the shell, holding it high in front of her. Then she slowly let it fall in a cascade of diamond droplets that glittered in the low light of the sun.

She handed the shell to Sedge to hold and began to speak. 'O River. Your otters call. We beseech you, Lady River, hear us, and listen.' She paused, swallowing hard.

This was the set part of the ritual – Sedge had heard these words often before, as he'd stood holding this same shell. There were ceremonies to sweeten the river every turning of the moon, though they were not always as grand as this one. He hadn't had to wear a stupid hat for a while. For all the usual ceremonies the words had been handed down, and all the otters had to do was repeat them.

But this time, his mother would have to leave the set words behind. With the waters rising far enough to flood the holt, and more rain coming, it was up to her to sing directly to the spirit of the river. It was the lady of the holt's most sacred duty to intercede on behalf of the otters whenever there was great need or danger. It was vital that she got it right, and for these ceremonies there were no instructions. Some of the previous lords and ladies of the holt had their songs written down afterwards, if they were particularly poetic, or if they'd actually worked.

The old books of the holt recorded tales of otters who had walked and talked with Lady River, and loved her as a second mother – or even as a friend. In those days the waters had run smooth and sunlit, filled with fish. The cubs were told stories about the river, stories that described her as an otter, her coat silvery-white and shining with moonlight. She was a mother like their own mothers, and though she cared for all the creatures of the water and the riverbank, she loved the otters most of all. The river of the old tales was gentle but strong; fierce but ever-giving.

Now the river seemed a strange, changeable creature, one who hardly listened to her otters at all. Sedge's mother had seen Lady River walking in the distance once, and swum after her, but she hadn't told Sedge what happened next. He still wasn't sure if she didn't know, or she just couldn't bring herself to describe being left behind.

He gripped the mussel shell tightly, wondering what she was going to say. She couldn't sound too desperate, not without sending the whole holt into a panic, but at the same time, she needed the river to hear how frightened they all were. She had to make the river hear them.

His mother's voice broke the listening silence at last. Her song was a hushed chant, barely loud enough to be heard over the rushing water, and the breath of many otters.

> *River. We beg you. The waters are rising,*
> *It's the springtime again,*
> *And my people are frightened.*
> *They see your waters seeping into our home,*
> *Your fingers reaching into our storerooms.*
> *We hear the claws of our enemies sharpened on*
>   *your stones.*
> *Please, O River . . .*
> *Be gentle.*
> *Draw your waters back,*
> *And show your loving otters some mercy.*

Sedge saw his mother's claws flexing on the hilt of her stone knife, as she bent her head to the water. She didn't sound loving, he thought. She sounded angry.

Since she had dragged Sedge back from the water the previous spring, Thorn's songs to the river had changed. The river had tried to steal her child, and she was supposed to plead for mercy? Thorn was still the lady of the holt, but she no longer sounded as though she expected the river to listen to her. There was no music in her singing now, and her voice stumbled and cracked as she carried on.

> *Or if you cannot do that,*
> *Lady River, come slowly.*
> *Creep onwards, and let us scurry back.*
> *Do not flood our holt again,*
> *We humbly ask you.*

Here she stopped and beckoned to a pair of small pups dancing from paw to paw beside her, so excited to be part of the ritual that Sedge guessed they hadn't listened to what the lady of the holt was saying. Each of them carried a woven willow basket, laden with flower petals, marsh marigolds like little flaming suns, and the deep velvet purple of irises.

His mother nodded to them, waving a paw at the water, and smiling sadly. The two cubs tossed the flowers out into the stream, so enthusiastically that one of them threw the basket too, and had to lean out and snatch it back in a hurry. Then they ran delightedly back to their parents, and the otters watched the petals swirl and eddy across the water.

Sedge fixed his eyes on one iris flower, so dark it was almost black, its petals slashed with yellow at the centre. It rushed onwards in the current, carried out to the deeper channel in the middle of the stream. The water was so fast – he forgot, sometimes, how strong the river could be.

He had thought that the ritual was over – he was about to turn away – but then his mother spoke again. Her voice was a mere breath of a whisper now, one that only the otters nearest to her could hear. The words were swept away on the soft splashing of the river almost as soon as she sang them.

No more.
No more from us.
No more from me.

Sedge stared at his mother, frightened by the depth of bitterness in her voice. Of course he knew that she was angry; that she felt the river had broken faith by stealing him away. But the river had given him back – couldn't his mother forgive, after all this time, for the sake of the holt?

It was spring again, Sedge thought, seeing the sharp glitter in his mother's eyes. The water was rising, and she was remembering the theft of her child. His mother's anger seemed to seethe around him, and dark thoughts swirled inside Sedge.

Dark thoughts, and darker memories, long held back. Sedge staggered a little, his hind paws slipping on the muddy edge of the bank. He gripped the mussel shell so tightly that he felt its pearly edge slice his pad. Trying to stop himself shouting out in pain, he stared firmly at the trees on the other side of the bank. What was he seeing? He leaned forward, searching through the rushes . . . someone was there, looking for him . . .

A hiss of horrified whispering brought Sedge back to his senses, and he realised that his mother was staring down at him, her eyes aghast. All the otters of the holt were murmuring anxiously behind him, and one of the tiny pups who'd carried the flower baskets scurried to the edge of the bank to peer into the water.

'It's gone!' he squeaked, and Sedge blinked at him.

What had he done?

He rubbed his paws nervously against his tummy fur, and then he realised that his paws were empty, and of course they shouldn't be. He was supposed to be holding the mussel shell, the same finely carved mussel shell that the holt had been using for these ceremonies for so many seasons. Sedge peered down, hoping that he'd only dropped it by his hind paws, or perhaps put it safely on one of the tree roots that stretched out into the water.

'You dropped it in the river,' the cub told him, patting Sedge's fur with a small paw. And then, trying to be comforting, 'Never mind.'

It was his sweetness that sent Sedge plunging back through the crowd, scattering them like startled birds as he dashed for the holt. He couldn't just stand there, feel them all staring, and wondering, and worrying. *What did it mean*, they would be whispering, *to have lost the shell*? No one would let it be just a clumsy young otter who didn't think what he was doing. It would be a bad omen, a sign that something was wrong.

The holt was going to spend days and days chewing it over. It would probably mean a whole new ritual, Sedge realised with a tiny moan as he bundled himself into his bedchamber. He flung the stupid wreath into a corner, and burrowed into his bed of reeds, pulling the embroidered blanket over his head. Perhaps he could pretend to be ill. He could be ill until the moon turned, and maybe by then everyone would have forgotten what he'd done.

He moaned again, muffling the noise in the blanket. This was the kind of thing that would be whispered about for ever. And what if the water levels kept rising? It would be his fault! He had made everything worse.

'Please, Lady River,' he whispered into the reeds of his

bed – they had come from the river after all, couldn't they send his message back? *'Please . . .* it was just me being careless. My mother frightened me, and I forgot that I was holding the shell. She was lost, she was so angry, that was all I could feel. I couldn't feel the water there at all.

'Don't let me dropping the shell spoil the ceremony. It's only a shell, isn't it? It doesn't mean we otters love you any less. Please don't flood us again.'

He wriggled further into the reeds. 'Maybe you didn't even notice. There must be more important things . . . not that it's not important, of course it is, I only mean, you must have other things to worry about . . .'

Sedge didn't know if he was asking, or cursing, or begging for forgiveness, not any more. 'Oh, please, it was a mistake. I didn't mean to . . .' He kept on whispering, until the darkness and the sweet smell of dry reeds slipped over him, and he drifted to sleep.

Sedge dreamed. He was small, so small he hardly knew anything, except the smell of his mother and the earthy damp scent of the holt. He was curled up in the bedchamber sleeping, full of the fish that his mother had brought, happy and warm. He had no idea what was creeping along the holt's tunnels and chambers towards him. Creeping, and then suddenly rushing in a terrifying gallop and swirl. The floodwaters surged into the soft nest and swept him away almost before he was awake, and he went tumbling head over paws out into the roaring river.

Sedge was dreaming, but a tiny part of him seemed still to be awake, watching the scene. That part knew what was coming next.

He'd had this dream before, so many times. But the dreams were growing stronger now, more real. Alone in his bedchamber, he whimpered in his sleep, his paws scuffling at the reeds of his bed, then he stretched out, reaching for something, someone – his mother? He scrabbled and grabbed, but again and again his paws closed only on dream water. He could feel it filling him now, cold darkness down his throat and into his chest. He choked and spluttered and the blackness filmed across his eyes.

And then they snatched him, pulling him out of the water with wild cries, and he was carried to the bank. They rolled him back and forth, pushing the water out of him until he coughed himself sick on the scrubby grass. When he opened his eyes at last, everything was different.

CHAPTER FOUR

The Holt

Sedge woke the next morning with the choking threads of his dreams still wrapped around him. He lay gasping under his coverlet for a moment or two, trying to remember what had happened the night before. He had a strange sense that something had been lost, left behind in the water. That it was his fault.

He rubbed a paw wearily across his muzzle, fighting to remember. The shell from the ceremony. He remembered now. That must be it.

But the flood and that desperate time lost in the wild river had been many moons before, he realised, as his breathing slowed.

Sedge shook his head, trying to clear away the dream fog, and yawned. Then sniffed. Someone had left him breakfast. A bark plate was sitting next to his bed, and he picked it up eagerly. He'd not eaten the night before, and now his stomach felt painfully hollow. Trout, lightly pickled to a soft pink, and wrapped in wild garlic leaves. He gobbled the tangy little parcels gratefully and licked his claws clean. Food helped – he felt more awake, the watery nightmares fading.

He peered out of his chamber doorway, listening for the familiar sounds of the holt. There was no cheerful rumpus from the main hall, so breakfast must be over. The same someone who had brought food had decided to let him sleep late. By now, everyone would be about their daily duties – fishing, gathering plants, guarding the holt.

He should be fetching herbs from the riverside to make teas and salves. It was one of his regular morning tasks. But first, he had to find his mother.

Sedge brushed his paws over his fur in a hopeful sort of way and padded down the passageway with the empty plate. He slipped through the main hall – empty apart from a couple of older otters comparing long lists on reed paper – and out into the kitchen. He wanted to see as few other otters as possible, and there was a little back tunnel he knew he could use to go and find his mother. She was sure to be out on the bank somewhere.

Bramble the cook looked round as Sedge tried to leave the plate discreetly on the corner of a tree-trunk table. 'Wash it up!' he said, glaring, but then he saw Sedge eyeing up a bowl of wild strawberries and sighed. 'Go on. Eat them, they won't last. Those little morsels of trout aren't enough to keep a growing cub. But wash the plate first.'

Sedge dipped the bark plate in a bowl of steaming water, and then dried it off, adding it to a wobbly pile on one of the shelves that lined the kitchen chamber. Then he dipped a paw in the bowl of strawberries, and nodded gratefully to the cook, scuttling out before he could be given a job to do. There was always work in the kitchens, and Bramble even made Sedge's mother shell crayfish if she was passing through.

The kitchen tunnel opened out between a pair of twisted roots at the side of the ancient willow tree. Sedge peered cautiously over the top. He could see a few young otters having a fishing lesson, but the river was mostly empty.

As quietly as he could, he padded through the long grass, heading upstream under the willows. His mother and Teasel often wandered up the bank to plan together, and watch the river. He needed to talk to his mother – to tell her how sorry he was, not only for dropping the shell, but for running away and hiding. The damp ground sucked at his paws, and when he looked back, he could see river water pooling in his prints. There had been more heavy rain the night before.

There were quiet voices up ahead, and he peered forward through the shadows of the branches. There they were, his mother and Teasel, standing together on a fallen tree trunk that stretched out into the water. They were examining the twigs and leaves that had gathered round the tree, and watching the current.

'The bank's building up silt behind here already . . .' his mother said, wrinkling her muzzle.

He padded slowly towards them, almost hoping that they wouldn't notice him, and he could sneak away without having to apologise for the night before. But when his mother spotted him, she pattered back along the tree at once to rub her paws over his ears and nose his muzzle.

'Did you sleep well?' she asked.

Sedge hung his head. 'No – I dreamed . . .' He swallowed hard, wanting to talk to her about his dream and her song, and that terrifying coldness between her and the river – but he couldn't find a way to say the words. He shook himself. 'Mother, I'm so sorry about the shell. I didn't even see that I'd dropped it. Perhaps I could search for another? Teasel could show me how to carve it.'

Teasel jumped down beside them and opened up the woven rush pouch slung across her front. She pulled something out and handed it to Sedge, grinning. 'Don't drop it again. Took me ages to find.'

'You got it back!' Sedge gaped at her. 'How?'

'River currents, the same ones I spent weeks teaching you.' The grizzled old otter shook a paw at him. 'We know where things wash up, Sedge. You will too, one day. But for now, it's safe back. No more dreams.' Teasel patted him too, scrubbing the soft fur over his skull, and for once Sedge didn't try to pull away. He turned the shell over and over in his paws. It wasn't even chipped.

'Is it still bad luck that I dropped it?' he asked hesitantly, looking between them.

His mother sighed. 'Perhaps.' She lifted her shoulders. 'Or perhaps Lady River only saw a troubled pup standing on her bank, and didn't even notice that you'd lost a shell. Who knows.'

'Are you still angry with the river?' Sedge blurted out, then he looked away from his mother, not sure he wanted to hear her answer.

There was silence for a moment, and then Lady Thorn answered his question with one of her own. 'Is that why you dropped the shell? You were shocked that I was angry?'

Sedge nodded.

'When you inherit the holt . . .' His mother gazed out across the water, turning her paws over and over each other. 'There's a chance you'll see her – the river spirit. It's part of the ceremony. Did you know that?'

'Is she real then?' asked Sedge. 'A real otter?'

Thorn shrugged lightly. 'The old tales say she takes the form of an otter, since otters are her joy above all things. But lately, I've felt she's been retreating from us. I suppose the life of one small otter seems very short and insignificant to her. I – I find that hard to accept.

'When I was standing there last night, looking at the river and listening to the song, it seemed to me that perhaps she doesn't understand us any more. The river should care about her otters, every one of them. And she doesn't.' His mother sounded bitter now. 'Every ritual, every time I'm supposed to call her to us with a song, that gets in the way.'

Lady Thorn laughed sadly to herself, and Sedge pressed closer to her. He was not that much smaller than his mother, for all she called him 'little one'. His head only just fitted under her chin.

'Perhaps today would be a good day for a lesson on the lore of the river and the holt,' Teasel growled softly.

Sedge's mother nodded. 'I shall stay here.' She padded out on the fallen tree again. 'I think the water levels might be starting to go down . . .' she murmured, leaning over and dipping a paw into the fast-flowing river.

As he followed Teasel along the bank, Sedge turned back to look at her, at the way she clung to the tree, her paw in the water, and gazed so fiercely, so fixedly at the river rushing by.

One day, that would be him.

The holt's lore was recorded in an ancient and tatty-looking book, preserved with great care in a carved wooden chest. It stood on a shelf in a small room behind the gathering hall, surrounded by a parade of strange exhibits that past otters had thought worth keeping.

Sedge was supposed to be able to recite everything in it, which seemed particularly unfair, since there had been hundreds of lords and ladies of the holt before him. It stood to reason that the amount to learn got longer every time somebody died, and by now there were pages and pages of the stuff. It wasn't as if it was interesting either – lists of names, and how so-and-so had protected the holt from the Great Fish Shortage, or the night wolf sneaking along the riverbank. Teasel treated that sort of complaint as pure laziness, and Sedge had given up trying to persuade her. He didn't think Teasel listened very carefully when he recited though. He was sure he'd caught the old otter napping once or twice.

'Is there anything in the book of lore about Lady River?' Sedge asked, as Teasel reverently lifted down the box. 'Did any of the past ladies or lords of the holt write about seeing her? Does it say what she's like?'

'So many questions,' Teasel muttered, and Sedge realised that she was worried. Was it because she didn't know the answer, or she wasn't sure if she ought to share it? 'There are mentions,' she went on cautiously, 'of a silvery-white otter, very tall and beautiful. They say she seems to rise out of the moonlight on the water, or drift up from the foam where the river runs over rapids or a waterfall. But the mentions are very few – only the most noble and beloved of her otters ever have sight of her.'

'But my mother *is* noble,' Sedge argued. 'She works so hard for the holt, all the time. She's always off settling some argument, or worrying about the storerooms, or fussing about silt build-up. She's the best leader we've had in a long time, everyone says so. That's why . . .' *That's why it'll be so hard to follow after her*, he wanted to say.

Teasel seemed to know what he had been about to say. 'You will be a great leader too, young one. If you—'

'Concentrate on my lessons, I know.' Sedge sighed. He wasn't sure if it was really true. Learning all about the river would help, he supposed, but that couldn't be everything. There had to be more. His mother knew all the lore of the water, she was devoted to the holt, but the river had still broken faith with her.

'I was going to say, if you swear to do your utmost to protect your holt always. I don't mean swear it to us, but to yourself.'

'Oh . . .' Sedge brushed his paw over the book, not looking at Teasel. He wasn't sure what an oath like that even meant. It sounded deep and grand and wonderful. But frightening too. How could he be responsible for the holt, and everyone in it?

'Lady Rush recorded seeing the river spirit, I think,' Teasel muttered, interrupting Sedge's thoughts, riffling through the pages with her thick old claws. 'Yes, here . . .' She pointed at a page, written in spidery brown ink. 'Look, Sedge.' She tapped at the faded writing. 'Can you read it?'

Sedge squinted at the page sideways, and wrinkled his muzzle, trying to make out the faint words.

N THE DARK NIGHT OF WINTER, A SILVER-WHITE OTTER CAME TO LADY RUSH, RISING UP OUT OF THE DRIFTS LIKE A CHILD'S SNOW OTTER COME TO LIFE. SHE WAS WHITER THAN THE SNOW, AND SHINING, AND HER EYES WERE THE BLACK OF THE NIGHT. THIS WAS THE FIRST TIME THAT LADY RUSH HAD SEEN LADY RIVER, AND SHE WAS SORE AFRAID.

LADY RUSH COVERED HER EYES WITH HER PAWS AND BOWED LOW TO THE RIVER, BUT THE WHITE OTTER LIFTED HER UP, AND CALLED HER 'LITTLE COUSIN', AND 'MY DEAREST CUB'. SHE TOLD LADY RUSH THAT SHE WAS NOT TO BE AFRAID, FOR THOUGH THE WINTER WOULD BE LONG, THE HOLT WOULD BE SAFE AND WARM UNDER THE WILLOW TREE, AND IF THEY MELTED THE ICE BY THE FALLEN OAK UPSTREAM, THERE WOULD BE A FISHING HOLE WITH A RICH CATCH FOR HUNGRY OTTERS, ENOUGH TO FEED ALL HER NEEDY MOUTHS THROUGHOUT THE LONG SNOW.

SO LADY RUSH WENT TO THE FALLEN OAK, THOUGH MANY OF THE FISHERS IN THE HOLT TRIED TO COUNSEL HER THAT NEVER HAD A FISH BEEN CAUGHT UNDER ITS ROOTS. SHE HAD THEM MELT THE ICE, AND THERE THEY FOUND THE PLUMPEST FISH, HEAVY AND GOOD. THE HOLT REJOICED, AND WHEN THE THAW CAME, AND THE SNOW-WHITE CHERRY BLOSSOMS BEGAN TO STAR THE TREES, LADY RUSH GATHERED THE PETALS. THE OTTERS OF THE HOLT CAST THE WHITE FLOWERS ON THE RIVER, AS A GIFT FOR THE LADY OF THE RIVER IN HER SNOW-WHITE COAT.

Sedge blinked and glanced at Teasel. 'We do that!' he said. 'Last night, we threw petals. But not white ones.'

Teasel nodded. 'This is why you learn the book,' she growled. 'Our history is still part of us. As lord of the holt, that's something you must understand.'

Sedge nodded reluctantly. He supposed that Teasel was right, but he didn't see why someone hadn't just picked out all the interesting bits. Perhaps that would be his contribution to the holt, he thought, rather glumly. *The Shorter Chronicles of Greenriver.* At least lazy pups would remember him with gladness, even if no one else did. They could put it on his memory stone.

'Is there a stone for Lady Rush?' he asked Teasel.

Teasel turned to look at the tall cairn built across the far end of the room, where the stones were piled so high that they almost covered the back wall of the chamber. 'I've seen it,' she muttered. 'I know I have. Now, where was it . . . far down, it must be . . .'

She crouched, peering along the lower rows of stones, and Sedge followed her, blinking in the dim glow of the rushlight she held. It cast flickering shadows over the stones, so that the carved words seemed to dance and swim before his eyes like otters. *Bravest. Dear One of the River. Great Fisher. Counsellor.*

'Ah, here.' Teasel straightened up triumphantly and pointed at a stone a few rows up from the ground. It was old enough that the carved words had softened with time to faint shadows, and the stone itself was pinkish, flecked with sparks of white quartz like petals, or snow.

'*Lady Rush – greatly beloved of the River*,' Sedge read, sighing. He stood up on his back legs again, and then stretched to look at the topmost row of stones. There were a few names that he recognised – Ripple, the elderly grizzle-fur fisher who'd sat in the corner of the gathering hall for as long as Sedge could remember, until he slipped away as the days began to lengthen, and Beck, a young otter who'd caught a fever back in the winter and died despite the healers' ever more desperate efforts. Sedge read on, remembering most of the names. His own grandfather. An older aunt. But . . .

Sedge peered at the stones, looking for something though he was unsure what. He shivered, and cold claws closed around his gut as he imagined his own memory stone, set into the cairn.

Lost to the river. He could almost see it. He stroked a paw across the row of stones, chasing a memory, something so close. He could almost *touch* it.

'Here. Leave that,' Teasel muttered, hauling him away. 'Outside, you. No sense in stewing inside all day. Go and find the others.'

Sedge pulled away, blinking in surprise. He had been so close to remembering . . . something. But what?

And what had come over the old otter? Sedge usually had to beg to be allowed out to play with the others.

'Out, out,' Teasel growled, shooing him through the passageways, and Sedge tumbled out into the light and the singing sound of the river.

Whatever he'd been chasing was quite gone.

Teasel left him with a gang of younger otters who had been collecting crayfish for Bramble the cook. They were sneaking off from the kitchens before they were made to shell the fiddly things too.

'So . . . there's no more lessons for today?' Sedge asked doubtfully, and Teasel nodded, before wheeling away.

'What bit her?' pale-furred Lily asked, jerking her head at Teasel, who had darted off along the bank so fast she was practically scurrying.

Sedge shrugged.

'Who knows? I wasn't any more terrible than usual. Come on, let's swim. You want to play hide and seek?'

'Oh yes, Your Lordship. Whatever you say, Your Lordship,' sneered Pebble, Lily's older brother. 'Didn't know the lord of the holt got to choose our games now as well.'

'Shut up, Pebble,' Tormentil dipped her paw in the water and scooped a bright arc of drops at his speckled nose.

'You said you wanted to play hide and seek when we were hunting crayfish,' said Flint, one of the smaller cubs. Then he darted back behind Tormentil, looking surprised at his own daring.

'I've changed my mind,' Pebble muttered, but no one was listening. Tormentil had already rolled over and slipped into the water, and now the others were diving after her. Pebble was left hesitating on the bank, until at last he followed, plunging gracelessly into the river with a splash.

'Don't see why we have to have him along,' he growled, just loud enough for Sedge to hear. 'We all swim better than him. He'll slow us down. Some lord.'

Sedge pretended he hadn't heard. He didn't think he was that much slower than Pebble anyway. And he'd dived clean, only a few bubbles showing his path through the water.

They swam on downstream until they were too far from the holt to be called back.

'I'll seek first, you all go and hide,' said Tormentil, once all five of them had clambered out on to a mudbank. 'Only between the two oak trees. No cheating this time, Lily.'

Lily brushed her whiskers with one paw, trying to look innocent, but Sedge could see that she was smirking. He had missed out on all this – whatever Lily had done, and all the teasing afterwards. He had a sudden sharp twinge of jealousy, but he cast it away as Tormentil curled herself tightly into a clump of grass higher on the bank, and began to count, muffled but loud. 'Go on then! One . . . two . . .'

The otter cubs spurted away, Lily, Pebble and Flint dashing for their favourite holes and pools, while Sedge swirled uncertainly in midstream, listening to Tormentil's slow count, and wondering where to go.

The point of the game was to be found last of all, but the cubs weren't allowed to change their hiding places once they'd chosen them. They had all promised faithfully not to sneak out and hide again if Tormentil was coming too close. *Which means that everybody will, of course*, Sedge thought.

He turned again, watching a stream of bubbles as Flint darted under an overhanging bank. The shadows swallowed up the little cub, and Sedge had to blink and peer to see him at all, even though he knew Flint was there.

He paddled suddenly, furiously, downstream. He mustn't be found first. He'd never live it down.

He let the current carry him on, scanning eagerly for hiding places along the bank – he'd be at the oak tree soon, and then he'd have to turn back. He could hear Tormentil crying triumphantly that she was coming, and he dived under a mat of reeds and branches that had been swept along by the river and pushed up against the bank. He clawed a little space between the scummy weeds, his nose wrinkling with disgust at the smell. It would wash off, he decided. It was worth it – the flotsam couldn't be a regular hiding place, it had probably only been there a day or two. Tormentil might not think to look here.

He watched, snickering happily to himself, as Tormentil found little Flint – that overhanging bank had to be a well-known spot – and then Pebble, tucked inside a hollow tree on the bank. The big cub tried to wriggle away and argue that Tormentil had cheated somehow . . .

Only Lily was left now, but she was a wily one, Sedge reckoned, quiet and clever. She had dived under the surface and arrowed away as soon as Tormentil began to count. He wouldn't mind so much if she won – it might even be for the best. Pebble seemed bitter enough already. It would be wise not to make him resent his future lord even more.

He was concentrating hard on the view upstream, where he was sure Lily had gone to hide, and where Tormentil seemed to think she was too. Tormentil was quartering the stream, tracking back and forth, her whiskers trembling with frustration. Little Flint was watching from the bank now, snorting and chittering, twirling in ever more excited circles each time Tormentil drew a blank. Sedge peered out between the slimy twigs, watching Tormentil so intently that he didn't see – or hear – someone sneaking up behind him. He was taken completely by surprise when a heavy otter body thumped down on top of the mat of leaves, and big paws cuffed him sharply around the muzzle and ears.

'Aha! Got you!' It was Pebble, not Tormentil, crowing with triumph.

'Get off!' Sedge snarled. 'You're not seeker! Get off me!'

'Oi, Pebble!' Tormentil yelled from further upstream. 'Who said you could do that? I would have found him! You're cheating.'

'He was the one cheating,' Pebble roared, smacking Sedge down into the matted weeds again. 'It wasn't a fair hiding place. I was helping you out.'

Sedge spat out reeds and weed slime. 'It was fair! Only thing wrong with me hiding here is *you* didn't think of it first. Why shouldn't I hide under this stuff?'

'It's moving,' Pebble muttered shiftily. 'You've got to hide somewhere and keep still. That's the rules.'

'It's not moving! Bobbing about in the current, that's all. You just wanted a chance to get at me, didn't you?' Sedge advanced on Pebble, so angry that he forgot how much bigger the older cub was. He saw a grin spread over Pebble's face, splitting the big cub's muzzle. Clearly Pebble couldn't believe how lucky he was. The little rat Sedge was actually going to try and fight him?

Sedge gritted his teeth. He couldn't back down now; Pebble would never let him forget it. Better to slink back to the holt battered and aching than to be called a coward. He shoved Pebble in the chest with both paws. The older cub roared delightedly and jumped up, powering himself out of the water with his strong hind legs. He landed on Sedge like a hammer, mighty paws plunging him down among the broken mat of weeds, and deep into the silted river.

Sedge felt the breath pounded out of him, and his ears rang as he went swirling down through the water. For a moment he was too dazed even to gasp, but then his chest heaved and he fought for breath, his paws scrabbling frantically at the water. It seemed so heavy, it was forcing him down . . . there was a blackness behind his eyes, like ink, and it was threading out into the water . . .

'Sedge! Sedge!'

He coughed and blinked. He was being hit again, but they were smaller paws this time, patting anxiously at his muzzle, shaking him.

'There, he's awake, I'm sure I saw him breathe. Yes, yes, look. Sedge, wake up!'

Sedge blinked again, peering up into the fierce sunlight, shining down on him through the branches above. There were whiskered faces leaning over him too, their eyes dark and anxious.

'We thought you'd never wake up!' Lily gasped.

'Breathe slowly,' Tormentil ordered. 'Don't talk yet. You must have swallowed a lot of water.'

Sedge tried to sit up, but it was just too hard to move. He closed his eyes, feeling the strong glow of the sun press against the lids. The warmth was drying his sodden fur now. His muscles felt sodden too.

'Pebble . . .' he mumbled, and he heard Tormentil draw an angry breath.

'Stupid lout's disappeared. Too scared to admit what he's done, I suppose. He's lucky he didn't drown you! He'd have been exiled for sure. He might even be still, when we tell them what happened.'

Lily twisted her paws, turning them over and over, her

eyes full of worry. 'Our parents,' she whimpered, 'they'll be so angry with him.'

'No!' Sedge managed to sit up, wincing. 'No, you're not to tell. I don't want everyone –' he coughed, spluttering out a dribble of water – 'everyone knowing he beat me.'

'There's no shame in that!' Flint protested. 'He's a head taller than you and about twice as wide!'

'Please. It'll be the talk of the holt, how you had to rescue me. What will my mother think? Please, Tormentil? Please, Lily?' He was ashamed enough that the other cubs had seen; he couldn't bear it if the whole holt knew too. He could just imagine his mother pretending not to hear the whispers. The faces that Teasel would try not to make. He was a poor enough replacement for his mother as it was, without everyone knowing that Pebble could half drown him.

Lily rubbed at Sedge's damp fur, her paws busy squeezing out the water. 'You looked – you looked—'

'Just say it!' Tormentil snapped. 'He looked dead.'

Lily shivered. 'Imagine it – carrying him back, telling everyone that the heir was drowned.'

'But he isn't, Lily, so stop being so dramatic,' Tormentil said.

Sedge shuddered.

'Are you cold?' Lily asked.

'No,' he muttered. 'I was just thinking about the flood, the

Dark Spring. Of how my mother would have felt, seeing me carried back along the riverbank again.' They were staring at him, and he ducked his head, ashamed and angry with himself. He shouldn't have spoken of it. He wouldn't have, but he was light-headed and frightened and relieved and guilty all at once.

He'd reminded them of yet another thing that made him different and strange.

'Forget I mentioned it,' he whispered, head down.

But Lily pulled his chin up so that he was forced to look at them, her delicate paws under his muzzle, her eyes fixed on his. 'Why shouldn't you talk about the flood?' she asked him quietly. 'I would want to. It must have been so frightening, to be dragged back from the river like that.'

'We were only surprised because you never *do* talk about it,' Tormentil put in. 'And because . . .' she faltered, and glanced at Lily and Flint – as if there was something else she wanted to say, but she couldn't quite work out how.

All three of the young otters were looking anxiously at each other now. Flint had one paw in his mouth, nibbling uncertainly at his claws.

'What?' Sedge demanded, curiosity distracting him from the burning in his chest, and the loose tooth at the back of his jaw.

Lily sighed and patted his muzzle. 'Nothing. Tormentil didn't mean anything – only that we can't understand what it's like to remember that. Anyway, I'm sorry about my stupid brother. One of these days he's going to do something he can't wriggle out of. He frightens me.'

She did look frightened, Sedge thought. He would too, if Pebble were his brother – the bigger cub was so angry all the time. But there was something else going on. He'd seen her and Flint holding their breath, waiting for what Tormentil was going to say. Then they'd sighed, both of them, just a tiny little whisper of breath. They were relieved – or perhaps disappointed?

Whichever it was, Sedge was sure that Tormentil had been about to say something entirely different.

CHAPTER FIVE

The Stronghold, downriver from the Holt

Ripe black elderberries,
Gleaming in the sun,
Ripe black elderberries,
Enough for everyone.

Silken sang, the song twittering and fluting like a bird's, and then chuckled as she heard a reed bunting join in. It trilled the simple tune high up in a willow tree above her head and she raised her voice, adding a lower harmony as the bird carolled the high notes.

The reed bunting stopped singing at once, and Silken sighed. She hadn't meant to frighten it with her silly fancy – but no one at the lodge sang with her, not ever. It had seemed so right to weave the song together with the bird. It was stronger that way, it satisfied something deep inside her, something she hadn't even known she needed.

Slowly, uncertainly, the bird began to sing again, just a

few short trills, and then a pause. Silken could *hear* it listening, waiting for her to join in, and it filled her with delight. She closed her eyes, and let the notes sing out of her. The bird chirruped joyfully up above her, calling, 'Elderberries! Elderberries!' until Silken had to stop to laugh with how perfect it all was.

The reed bunting hopped down from branch to branch to peer at her, and chirped, 'Elderberries!' one more time, before fluttering away across the water in a puff of brown and white feathers. Silken watched it go, clutching her muddy paws against her chest, the warmth inside her fading away as she imagined what her father would have said.

She had been glad to escape that morning, sent out on a foraging day. The other young beavers thought of foraging as a chore, something to be avoided at all costs, but Silken loved the chance to swim and potter and rootle about along the riverbank. Besides, she wanted to be as far from the holt as possible, away from the gossip and the anger.

She had sat in the hall at supper the night before, trying to hide behind Frost – he was large enough, after all. But when she got up to head for bed, there was a moment of stillness as the beavers watched her go. Silken had glanced back as she reached the door to the bedchambers, and all she could see in the rushlights were a hundred glittering eyes.

It was time to make for the lodge; she could tell from the way the afternoon light was golden and gleaming on the water. She had a good store of clay burrowed out now, the strong thick kind that baked hard. She was just wrapping it in large leaves for the journey back, when a high, keening call brought her head snapping up. A beaver call, but one she hadn't heard for months. It went on and on, then broke and faltered as if whoever was calling had run out of breath. Silken heard a long, huffing gasp, and then the cry came again, over and over.

The lodge sent someone out on watch each morning and evening, a beaver who stayed on guard at the far limits of the clan's territory. It was their job to raise the alarm if there was a danger to the lodge, flooding perhaps, or some sort of an attack. The warning cry was for all the beavers out harvesting or wooding away from the lodge. It meant *Get back to the safety of home, as fast as you can.*

Silken had heard the call before, but only from the safety of the lodge. She had never been caught outside, in danger. She cast a hunted, frightened look up and down the bank. There had been no wolf sightings for many a moon. The beavers had started to hope that she was gone – settled somewhere upstream, or perhaps even dead. The creature was old enough, and she had that limp. It was part of what made her so dangerous though – that she was desperate.

Silken finished wrapping the leaves with shaking paws, making a bad job of it, and shoving the clay inside her bag anyhow. Then she slipped into the water and swam as fast and as quietly as she could towards the great river.

It was hard to stay undercover in the shallow stream. She had to keep half surfacing and scurrying along. She didn't know what the danger was, and that made her more frightened, not less. Last time the call had been a false alarm, a flood surge that hardly even lapped the dam by the time it had reached the lodge. Frost and Speckle had pointed out the heavy rainfall and the high river over the last few days – perhaps another flood surge was coming, a dangerous one this time. Silken shivered. She had never been caught out in a surge, but even the thought of it made her feel sick and cold inside.

Silken reached the mouth of the stream and peered around anxiously – was she in time? Out in the middle of the great river, a dark head was sailing by, carried along by the current. The watch guard, on her way back to the lodge, swimming as furiously as she could now that she had raised the alarm.

Silken was just about to shoot out into the main river – she could catch up with the watch guard, perhaps – when she realised what had made the guard call the alarm. She must have been caught unawares, since they were practically on her tail. No wonder the guard was paddling for her life.

Just rounding the bend in the river was a massive raft. Silken had never seen anything like it before, but she knew immediately what it was – something only a little less terrifying than the old wolf. She had heard so many stories, whispered by older members of the clan, told to frighten the little ones into good behaviour.

Be good, or the raft creatures will steal you away.

You watch out now! Any more of that and I'll be selling you to the rafters when they come by!

Come back here, little one. You go too far and one of those nasty rafters will snap you right up . . .

The raft was made of massive tree trunks all lashed together, with bundles and crates tied on. In the middle was a strange arrangement of woven cloth, strung around thin poles. *Some sort of shelter*, Silken thought. In and out and all around the poles darted creatures that Silken had never seen before – but she knew who they must be.

Otters.

Silken huddled close to the bank, ducking under a clump of dangling roots. It was too late to chase after the guard now, too late to race for the lodge. She was on her own.

She watched the raft sail closer, her paws growing cold on the tangle of roots. She could see them clearly now, the creatures on the raft. They were tall, and long-tailed, with smooth, close brown fur, much shorter than a beaver's. Most of them seemed to be wearing knives, the sheaths slung across the body on a belt.

Many of the stories she'd heard about otters – especially *these* otters, the traders, who roamed up and down the river, swaggering and sneaking and stealing – ended the same way.

Now, don't you ever let those otters get their paws on you. They want your skin, you know. To make themselves a little beaver-skin hat. You stay well out of their way, small one.

One of the otters was using his blade to gut a silvery fish now, tossing the innards out into the river. But in spite of the knives, the otters didn't *look* like the sort of creatures that would make hats out of her. There were two small ones, chasing each other all over the raft, over the boxes and bundles, even into the water. Silken watched as one leaped in, squeaking and splashing, and the other jumped gleefully after. The pair of them paddled rapidly around the raft and scrambled back on – and then they did it again.

When old Grizzle had told them about otters, even the settled otters who lived in some kind of dirty hole further up the river, she had made them sound fierce. Great big teeth, she'd said they had, as well as the knives, and sharp ripping claws. To Silken, the otters' claws looked about the same size as a beaver's. Their teeth, to be honest, were smaller. A bit more pointed. They ate fish mostly, Silken knew, her gaze drifting back to the otter with the knife.

The two little otters were wrestling in the river now, turning over and over. One would wriggle away, and then set up a great splashing and sneak back up on the other under cover of the sparkling water.

The raft was pulling ahead though – the great tall otter poling it along hadn't noticed the little ones dropping behind. Silken watched them anxiously, much as she'd watch Brindle and Soft-ears and the smallest beavers when they were playing in the water.

She wasn't that frightened any more, she realised. Her paws weren't icy, and her heart had stopped hammering. She was enjoying watching those two small ones, and she wanted to know more about the raft, and what was in all those boxes and packages piled up. She couldn't ask, of course. If she let them so much as see her, they'd all have their knives out in a flash. But still . . . perhaps she could swim after them a little way? If she was careful to keep out of sight.

Then the otter poling the raft looked back and roared, 'Watch it, you two! Get yourselves back along here, right now!' He stuck the pole down hard into the river bed to anchor the raft against the current.

The two small otters turned at once, and began to paddle neatly and quickly towards the raft. They didn't look that upset about being told off though; Silken could see them giggling.

'Oh, you may laugh now,' the bigger otter growled. 'But we're just coming up on the lodge, did you know that?'

The two small ones scrambled up on to the raft at once, looking around worriedly, and one of them pressed herself tight against the big otter's side. Her fur was all sticking up in wet spikes.

'Exactly,' the big otter said, his voice so low and grim that Silken had to strain to hear him. 'Stay on board now. I want you two with me. Not a tail's length away, you understand? I don't trust those creatures, and I want you where I can see you while we're passing the dam.'

Those creatures? Silken forgot herself enough to lean out around the tumbling roots.

And did he mean *her* lodge? The beaver lodge?

Were . . . were otters as scared of beavers as beavers were of them?

Silken clung to the tree roots, gazing wide-eyed after the raft. It was something she had never even considered. Everyone knew that otters were bad. Nasty, tricksy, fierce and mean. They stole little beavers away to make hats. She had never wondered what otters might say about *them*.

84

'Now, don't look like that.' The big otter reached down one paw and patted the tiny one clinging to his fur. 'I'm only saying to be careful. We'll be past them soon, so you just stay here on the raft and huddle down among the cargo till we tell you, hmmm?'

Both small otters tucked themselves carefully between the boxes, so that Silken could only see a paw and the edge of whiskers. One of the other adults went to curl up close by, murmuring gently to them. Then the tall otter twisted the pole up out of the river bed, and set to driving the raft downstream again.

As he swung the pole up and in once more, he began to sing, and the other otters scattered round the raft joined in, the two cubs adding their high, squeaky voices.

On we go along the swirling river,
Onwards rushing on the tide,
Our craft is strong, and carries us so bravely,
So merrily again we ride . . .

The otter's low, rather gruff voice was nothing like Silken's, and the song was different from hers too, rich and brave, clearly meant to hearten the little otters hiding by his feet. Still, there was something about the song, the singing. It felt . . . familiar. The fur rose up on the back of her neck.

Silken watched silently as the raft slipped on down the river, straining her ears to catch the last faint notes of the song as the otters disappeared out of sight.

Something was twisting and pulling inside her. She knew that song. It wasn't just that it reminded her of her own singing, she was sure she had heard it before.

The wake from the raft rippled away to nothing against the knot of roots, and Silken climbed out of the stream and on to the bank. She crouched there, thinking fiercely, trying to drag back that thin memory of song. It was buried deep down inside her. The notes rose and fell in the same way her own songs did – the way that the other beavers found so strange and haunting.

Why did *she* sing the way an otter did?

Silken flinched as she heard the birds begin to chirp again on the other side of the river. The raft otters had scared them silent, but now that raft was well out of sight, there was a rush of excited twittering. Among the chatter she could hear one bird – no, maybe two now – singing, 'Elderberries! Elderberries!' The song was scattering onward, the words mangled but the tune twittering on up the river.

Silken wriggled a little forward, and peered down into

the clear water of the stream. There was a breeze, and tiny ripples raced across the surface – all she could see of herself was a blurry brownish head. Like any other beaver.

Then the wind dropped, and in that moment of still calm, Silken gazed at her own reflection in the water. A small, neat face stared back at her, with round black eyes, tiny ears and a fall of white whiskers. A long, lithe body and stout paws. She flicked her tail round, and saw it reflected in the water, full of muscle.

Suddenly frightened, Silken leaned in and swept a paw across the surface, scooping the picture away. She didn't want to look.

Silken had spent so long worrying that she was too thin, that her tail was different, that her hind paws weren't webbed enough. She'd wished and wished for teeth that could bite through a branch in moments, like Frost and Speckle.

She'd never, not once, considered that she didn't look like a proper beaver because she wasn't a beaver at all.

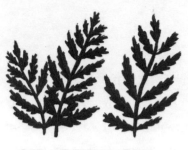

CHAPTER SIX

The Holt

Sedge woke, gasping. He sat up, wrapping his paws around himself tight, tight. His breath was a low wheeze as he tried to push away the dark, churning water of his dream. It was always the same – he was clutching desperately at an outstretched paw . . . reaching for something that he didn't understand.

He hadn't realised how exhausted he'd been, after the fight with Pebble. Lily and Tormentil and Flint had tried to persuade him to go to the healers for a balm for his bruises, a tincture for his bubbling lungs, but Sedge had refused. He'd soothed them all away, promising that all he needed was to be left alone.

Uncertainly, they'd let him go. He couldn't bring himself to creep back through the main chamber limping and battered, so he'd hidden up around the back of the holt, in a shadowy hole among the tree roots. He hadn't meant to fall asleep. His muscles were set stiff now, and he felt cold to the bone in the evening chill.

'What's the matter with you?' Teasel demanded, stomping past Sedge sitting in among the willow roots. How did she always turn up whenever he least wanted her? 'Rain sick? Aren't we all. Get yourself up and doing something, laddie, don't just sit there.'

Sedge nodded and stood up.

'What is it?' Teasel asked, more gently this time. 'That look isn't just damp fur. What's wrong?'

Sedge stared at her in surprise. He was so used to Teasel shouting at him, it was almost more worrying when the grizzled old otter tried to be kind. 'It's nothing. Don't worry,' he said.

'You want me to tell your mother you're miserable?'

'No!'

'You'd better tell me then. You looked . . . broken-hearted there for a moment.' Teasel pushed him back down into the hollow among the roots and settled next to him. 'Talk.'

'It was only that I had a dream,' Sedge said, horribly embarrassed. 'You don't want to hear about my dreams.'

She wrinkled her muzzle. 'No, I don't. But then again, we all have them. *Are* you broken-hearted, laddie? You're young, to be thinking of a mate.'

Sedge looked up in horror, his whiskers quivering. 'Not a dream like *that*!'

Teasel sighed exasperatedly. 'So what sort of dream was it, youngster? Spit it out!'

'It was about the Dark Spring.' Sedge beat his paw against the willow roots. 'I don't remember it but I dream about it all the time. Why can't I remember? It's all there, somewhere. It has to be, or how could I dream it? There's something I'm missing, I know there is, and it's important. I need to remember! It's just . . . there . . . but I can't reach it.'

'Ah.' Teasel was silent for a moment.

'You were in the dream too,' Sedge whispered. 'You pulled me out of the water.' He huddled closer in to the roots, gazing out across the river.

'You shouldn't dwell on such things, young one,' Teasel muttered uncomfortably. 'Best to put it out of your mind.'

Sedge looked at her, bewildered. How was he supposed to do that?

'No point looking back.' Teasel patted Sedge's shoulder, but she wouldn't meet his eyes. She seemed jumpy, and worried, as she had been after their lesson that morning. 'I must get on,' she said hurriedly. And before Sedge could ask what the matter was, she got to her feet again and darted away, hopping hurriedly from root to root until she disappeared in the back door.

Sedge sat there for a moment longer, confused and

disappointed, and then he wriggled out of his little root nest and slipped into the water. The rain was pattering pleasantly on the river, turning it silver-grey with rings of ripples. Once he was below the surface, he could see the shimmering shocks of rain dancing down through the water, bright notes that chimed like otter voices. It was soothing. Sedge arrowed out to a deeper pool, a way downstream from the holt, and began to coil himself in long, slow spirals. It was a trick he could do without conscious effort, and it left his mind free to think. To remember.

'There you are. We've been looking for you for ages.'

Lily and Tormentil slumped down beside Sedge on the bank, one on either side of him, and Lily groaned.

Sedge blinked at her.

'What's the matter?' he asked Lily.

He'd worn himself out swimming, trying to pull the memories up to the surface, and then he'd had to scramble out on to the bank to rest and groom. He was still half wrapped in his thoughts of the flood, and it was hard to bring himself back to the damp riverbank. Someone was reaching out to him still, their paws almost touching. Someone so familiar.

How could he not know who it was? They were there on the riverbank, almost more real than Lily and Tormentil . . .

'Your mother,' Lily moaned, scuffing her claws in the grass and raking up the dark earth below.

Tormentil hissed a warning, and Lily's eyes widened.

'Sorry, Sedge. I didn't mean . . .'

Sedge only shook his head. He was waking up a little now. That strange dark-furred dream otter was fading away. 'It doesn't matter. What's she done?' he asked Lily curiously.

'We shouldn't complain about her to you. Or to anyone!' Tormentil said disapprovingly. 'She's the lady of the holt. She's your *mother*.'

'Tormentil, stop fussing.' Lily sighed. 'Your mother says we need a new song for the next full moon ceremony. A special one, to do something to the water levels.'

'To *abate* them,' Tormentil said, in a voice that sounded scarily like Sedge's mother. She eyed the river lapping at the bank. The grey water was swirling closer than it should be, and the grass was spongy wet under their paws. 'She says it's been raining for too long, and there's no signs of it stopping. I think everyone's worried that it's even worse than last spring. The old otters keep saying that they've never seen such strange weather.'

'And the song needs to send away the night wolf,' Lily put in.

Sedge turned to her. 'The night wolf?' he said, hearing the squeak in his voice.

'Didn't you hear?' Lily asked. 'Bramble threw a load of fish scraps out of the back door last night, and he was sure he saw something watching from the other side of the river. He's been telling everyone who even sets a paw in the kitchens. He says it was huge. Anyway, this new chant's very long, and very complicated, and we have to sing a terrible lot of it.' Lily shook her head. 'We'll never get it right.'

'There's a while to practise though,' Sedge pointed out. 'The moon's just starting to wane now.'

'It's not long enough,' Lily growled. 'We're never going to have the chant learned in time, it goes on for ever.'

'It's hard to sing,' Tormentil admitted. 'All the parts sort of wind round each other.'

He should probably go and find his mother, or Teasel, Sedge thought. There would be words to learn. All the otters would join in creating the perfect spell to cast across the rising waters, and as heir to the holt, his part was bound to be important and difficult. But Sedge was starting to doubt that the otters' songs and ceremonies would ever still the river. How could they, when his mother was so full of anger, and disappointment and sadness? She had said the river wasn't listening . . .

Sedge sighed. She didn't have a choice but to keep trying, he supposed. She couldn't admit to her otters that the ceremonies meant nothing. If she did, they would know that the holt wasn't safe any longer. It was bad enough that otters were already sneaking off in the night, as Teasel had reported; it would only get worse now that there were whispers about the night wolf stalking the riverbank too, ravening with hunger. If the otters didn't trust that his mother and Lady River would protect them, then the holt would be deserted in days.

Sedge nibbled his claws and gazed out across the water, hardly hearing his two friends practising snatches of the ceremonial chant, beating their paws on the muddy bank for time.

'Ugh.' Lily slumped over on to her back, staring up at the dark-grey sky. 'I give up. Even the weather's making me sad.'

'That's the point.' Tormentil snorted, and pushed her, and then the two of them rolled over together in a mock-fierce scuffle, snapping and hissing until they collapsed back on the grass, worn out.

Then they leaned over the rising water, dabbling their paws, and began to sing again. Not the slow, sad chant this time, but one of the old ones they loved. Sedge listened to them, humming along as they moved from song to song, and thought about the water seeping slowly up around the holt.

A sweet, eerie thread of music jolted him back, and he whipped his head round, staring at Tormentil and Lily.

'Where did you hear that?' he bit out. The two cubs gazed back at him in surprise.

'We heard the birds singing it,' Tormentil said. 'The little warblers in the reeds last night.'

Lily nodded. 'We couldn't make out the words – you know how they babble – but it's catchy.'

It was catchy – more to the point, it was intensely, suddenly familiar. Sedge could have sung the words to Lily and Tormentil, or he could have if his voice hadn't been stuck fast in his throat.

> *Ripe black elderberries,*
> *Gleaming in the sun,*
> *Ripe black elderberries,*
> *Enough for everyone.*

A tide of memory slammed into Sedge, sending him back into his dreams, twisting and turning in the dark floodwaters again. She was there, teeth bared and eyes stretched wide in panic, reaching out her paws to him. Sedge was struggling in the water, trying desperately to catch hold of her. They were so close, but the water kept tearing them apart.

His sister.

Elderberry.

The song that Lily and Tormentil were chuckling over was hers. Elderberry had first made it on this same stretch of bank, kicking her paws in the water with him. They were too young to have tasted fresh elderberries, of course, since they were a late summer fruit, but Bramble had enough of them preserved and pickled in clay jars in the storerooms. Elderberry jam – he could taste it now. His sister had been expert at charming spoonfuls out of the old cook.

His sister.

Hearing that song again unleashed a torrent of memories that raced through his head as violently as the flood. Sedge sat shaking on the wet grass, bewildered and frightened. She had been there waiting for him all this time.

How could he have forgotten her?

Elderberry's paw patting affectionately at his muzzle.

Chasing her along the bank and in and out the kingcups.

The first full moon ceremony where they'd stood together, draped in garlands, half asleep by the end.

The stories she'd told him as they sunned their fur on a dry bank.

Their swimming lessons . . .

She had looked so bright, dashing about in the shallows, whipping up the sparkling water with her tail. The memory was so strong, he felt he could reach out his paw and touch her, twine his tail in hers. She had been merry, alive.

Except of course she wasn't. The river had stolen her away, and only Sedge had been left coughing and choking on the bank. He had let her go.

This was what he had been fighting to remember all this time. Sedge twisted his paws together, over and over. But how could he have forgotten in the first place? Why had he been *allowed* to forget her? Had he hit his head, when he was in the water? Or had it simply been too much for one small otter to hold inside his heart?

He remembered *everything* now. He could see his mother, running up and down the riverbank, her voice hoarse with screaming for his sister. He'd curled terrified and guilty in Teasel's arms, watching her, sure that somehow it was his fault.

After all, he'd lived. Elderberry hadn't.

'The birds were singing that song?' Sedge forced out at last. He couldn't look at Lily and Tormentil.

He hadn't heard it since that last night, when they were curled together in their tiny bedchamber in the holt, the night the waters came. It was the song that Elderberry sang to him when they were falling asleep, their own special song. She had made a second verse, just for him.

Pale dry sedge grass,
In the wind it sings,
Pale dry sedge grass,
Whispers secret things.

Sedge could hear the grasses on the riverbank whispering it to him now, laughing as the wind hissed by. He ached to sing it out loud again.

But how did the birds know *his* song?

Lily eyed him curiously. 'Yes. Do you know the song then?'

He had forgotten it entirely – and even if he had remembered it, he would never, ever sing it aloud, not now, not with Elderberry gone. So who had heard it? Who had sent it echoing up the river? Elderberry had sung that song all the time, chirping it as she combed his fur, or pottered around their bedchamber, but only when it was just the two of them.

Who had sung it, now that Elderberry was gone?

Sedge swallowed. 'I must have heard it somewhere,' he said, and Lily shook her head at his strangeness, and went back to singing with Tormentil. The bright tune danced around them, stirring up so many forgotten things.

Supper had never seemed to last so long. All Sedge wanted was to get to his bedchamber, to be alone and think through everything he'd learned.

He slipped away as soon as the main meal was over, ducking out of the stories and songs with a muttered excuse to Teasel. His old teacher eyed him sharply, but waved him on.

Sedge hurried through the holt and flung himself into the room, closing the door with a tiny thump. He breathed. Then he stretched out a paw to the shelf above his bed of rushes and lifted down a carved wooden box. It had treasures in it: a feather or two, some sweet dried herbs, a pebble he'd found that glittered golden. He sifted through the keepsakes and picked out a woven cord, strung with a small yellow-white tooth. Someone had given it to him, but he'd never worn it – the cord felt itchy, and why would he want to wear one of his own baby teeth anyway? It made sense that his mother wore one, it was a sentimental thing. For him to wear something like that was only odd.

He held the tooth in his paw and studied it, rubbing the smoothness against his pad. It wasn't his, he knew that now. It was Elderberry's tooth, and he had been given it to remember her by. It hadn't worked.

He could feel his mother dropping the itchy cord around his neck – another thing he'd chosen not to remember. Slowly, the cord sliding in his shaking paws, he pulled it over his head, and everything seemed to slip into place.

There were two things he knew.

Elderberry was still alive. Her song had travelled up the river, and that meant that she was there, somewhere downstream. He was sure of it.

The second thing he knew was that it was up to him to go and find his sister. No one else would believe him. Not his mother, not Teasel. They wouldn't understand what that song meant. No one could. No; *he* had to be the one to go. Sedge picked up the leather belt that carried his knife. He didn't need anything else. He allowed himself a moment to dream as he buckled the belt on. He would find his sister and bring her back to the holt – to his mother!

Sedge's paws stilled on the buckle as he understood at last. No wonder his mother was so angry with the river, when the rising waters had stolen away both her babies. Should he ask her about it? He could go back to the hall, and talk to her, he could reassure her . . . But he wouldn't be able to explain the certainty, the deep knowledge inside him that Elderberry was still alive. They would be gentle, pitying. They would explain all over again that she was gone . . .

Sedge pressed the tooth tighter in his paw, so tight he could feel the point cutting into his pad.

How happy, how proud would his mother be, if he could bring back her lost child. She would be able to love Lady River once more. And if his mother could sing to the river without that burning loss, then surely the waters would go down. Elderberry could add her sweet voice and skill at weaving songs to their mother's, and perhaps Sedge could even find his own voice again. The three of them would sing to Lady River together.

The older otters wouldn't be sighing and shaking their heads over him any more. And Pebble! So what if Pebble was bigger? Sedge would have rescued his sister – the holt's true heir! – and driven back the flood, while Pebble had only wasted his time in silly fights.

Sedge could feel the excitement bubbling like a waterfall inside him as he opened the door to his bedchamber and peered out into the dark passageway. It would be *easy* to ignore the message that the song had sent up the river, easy to plod on with the daily ache of lessons and study and training and ritual.

To be a true son of the holt, he had to leave it. It was his duty.

He'd never had a duty he liked the sound of more.

CHAPTER SEVEN

The Stronghold

Silken backed away from the water, and sat shaking on the bank. How had she never worked it out before? All those times she had felt so different. Because she *was* different.

She couldn't be an otter. She was *scared* of otters. Everyone was! Otters were fierce and mean and murderous. Otters weren't quite as frightening as the old wolf, nothing could be, but they weren't far behind.

Silken stretched out her paws in front of her and stared at them. An otter's paws. A stranger's paws.

She looked over her shoulder at her tail – the tail she had worried about so much, long and pointed and furred, not flat and scaly like the others. Looking at it now, she felt foolish. It was so obvious that she wasn't the same sort of creature, but the thought had never entered her mind.

A great shiver ran through Silken as she realised something else. If she wasn't a beaver, then of course her father wasn't her father either.

Nothing he had told her was true. Her mother – the green woven scarf – it had nothing to do with Silken at all. Somehow this hurt more than anything. Silken curled herself into a ball, pulling her tail in tight. He had lied to her for all this time.

She had been thinking of leaving anyway, since the day Tawny had attacked her, when she had seen the strange, dark looks on the faces she had grown up with. Of course, thinking back on what Tawny had said, she should have realised then that something was wrong.

Since you call her your daughter.

She'd been too upset to pay attention at the time, but now it made sense. Did everyone know, then, that she wasn't her father's daughter? It must be common knowledge, at least among the older beavers; but surely Frost and Speckle didn't know. Silken couldn't imagine Frost having the tact to pretend.

She gave a little groaning cough of distress and pulled her paws over her head, tucking in tighter.

Could she trust her father to tell her the truth if she asked him now?

Silken could only think of one creature who might tell her. In the quiet, secretive life of the lodge, he was the only one welcomed from the outside. Silken's father himself had spoken of consulting him about Silken's strange singing. Her father had always spoken of him as a truth-teller, as one who could be trusted to pass on the news of the river. And he was old, very old. He would know what had happened, surely.

The swan.

She could leave now and find him.

It would be better than going back to the lodge, knowing that she didn't belong and that she never had.

Silken uncurled, eyeing the river. She pulled off the strap of her collecting bag, and shook the leaf-wrapped ball of clay into the water with a splash. There was no point in carrying it, if she wasn't going back. Her paws shook as she clutched the empty bag tight against her. It was all she had now. Just a woven reed bag.

It took almost until sunset, but at last, Silken reached the tall grove of silver birches she was aiming for, some way upstream from the lodge. The birch trunks glowed ghostlike in the dying light, and the rich green leaves glistened and whispered as she arrowed towards the patch of bank that she remembered.

The nest was at the very edge of the water, surrounded by thick clumps of reeds. It was huge, at least three times as wide across as Silken herself. And it was empty.

Silken climbed up, peering into the mass of reeds and twigs. The middle of the nest was softer than the sides, made of finer grasses, and dotted with white belly feathers. Silken perched there uncertainly. The riverbank seemed silent; the only sounds were leaves fluttering on the trees and the faint lap of water against the nest. She sniffed at the dry reeds cautiously, wondering how long it was since the swan had been here. Perhaps the old nest had been abandoned?

Then she heard something – a low, thumping noise. She pressed herself against the side of the nest. The sound was heavy and rhythmic and getting louder, and she couldn't work out what it meant. Then across the width of the sluggish river came an angry scream, and Silken realised – too late – that the rapid thuds were wingbeats. The swan was coming back, and she was perched on his nest.

'Out! Out!'

He looked far bigger than he had when she was a tiny kit – how was that possible? His wings seemed to stretch halfway across the river, blocking out the light as Silken cringed against the pile of reeds. She was too frightened to move, even as he began to beat at her with those great white wings.

After a moment though, the swan seemed to realise that the interloper wasn't fighting back. He mantled his wings, closing Silken in a cave of white, and snaked his long neck round to peer at her suspiciously.

'What are you?' he hissed.

Silken lifted her head and looked back at him. 'I don't know,' she whispered.

'There are no otters in this part of the river,' the swan snarled. 'Where have you come from? Are you a spy?' He snapped his beak at her, and Silken squeaked and cowered back.

'A strange little spy,' the swan said, and she saw that he was amused.

'Do you – do you think I'm an otter then?' she asked him, all in a gasp.

The swan lowered his wings, staring at her. 'What else would you be?'

'I don't know,' Silken said, her voice very small.

The swan was silent for a moment, and then he folded his wings and settled into the middle of his nest, coiling his neck down to examine her properly. 'Where did you come from?' he demanded again.

'I – I was down the river,' Silken said.

'Downstream? Not up? You're not from Greenriver?' the swan questioned, still inspecting her, turning his head this way and that to see her with both eyes.

Silken scrambled closer, forgetting his beady eyes and threatening wings. 'Greenriver? Is that where the otters come from?'

The swan reared up, hissing. 'If you're not from Greenriver, you must be from some faraway holt. What are you doing here?' He brought his head right down next to hers. 'Get away,' he snarled. 'You shouldn't be in this part of the river, whatever you are. Get yourself home.'

Silken shuddered. 'I don't have a home.'

'You're an exile then? An outcast? No one wants you here either!'

Silken blinked at him, bewildered. Perhaps she was an outcast; she didn't know. 'I might be an exile,' she said pleadingly. 'But whatever I did that was wrong, that got me cast out, it must have been before I can remember. I've been at the Stronghold all my life. Or I thought I had.'

The swan went still, peering at her.

'An otter child, growing up in the beavers' lodge,' he muttered, and he fluttered his wings uncomfortably. 'Not yet full grown.' He brought his head down close to examine her again. 'Still small. Are you last spring's brood then?'

'Yes!' Silken said eagerly. 'At least, I think so. Do you know where I came from? My father never told me I wasn't his true child, and I didn't know where else to go, or who to ask. He said you knew everything,' she added, trying to flatter the old swan, hoping it would work. 'He wanted to ask you about me.'

'You should go back to your lodge.' The swan turned away from her and tucked his head under one of his great wings. 'Nothing to do with me,' he muttered, the words muffled by feathers.

'But it isn't my lodge!' Silken took another step further into the nest. 'I must have been brought to the Stronghold. If I'm not a beaver, I can't have been born there, can I? Didn't you ever hear anything about a foundling child on the river?'

'Stop bothering me!'

The swan sounded different now – still angry, but embarrassed too. Uncomfortable.

'You do know something,' she said slowly. 'Why won't you tell me?' She sighed. 'Is it because you think I won't like it? I want to know, truly, whatever it is you have to tell me. I promise I'll go, if you do.' She crept closer. 'And if you don't tell, I'll stay here.'

The swan surged upright, hissing like a boiling pot on a fire, and mantling his great wings again. Silken was hard put not to dive out of the nest and into the water, but she held her ground. 'Tell me what you know!' she demanded.

'And then you'll go?' he said.

'I promise.'

He settled back into the nest, fluffing his feathers, nibbling at a few, fussing and clicking his beak. It was like her own nervous grooming, Silken thought, watching him; something to do when one was uncomfortable.

Eventually he murmured, 'I remember you. Though you're larger now, of course.'

'I came here with my father once,' Silken told him. 'Except he isn't my father. He was asking you about the snow, back in the winter, when he was worried that the cold wasn't letting up.'

'No, before then, I knew you,' the swan told her. 'When you were very small.' He hesitated, and then he added quietly, 'I was the one who found you.'

'You!' Silken surged closer, laying one paw on the swan's neck. 'What do you mean, you found me? Where? What happened?'

The great bird wheeled back, hissing angrily, and Silken shrank away.

'I'm sorry, I'm sorry!' She took a deep, shaky breath and tried to speak more calmly. 'Tell me, please. Where did you find me?'

'Here.'

Silken looked around, confused.

The swan snorted bitterly. 'This isn't the first time you've sat in this nest, little one. I found you here last spring. This very spot.'

'In your nest?' Silken whispered, looking around at the darkening water. There was a faint golden-red glow through the birches now, but that was all. It was almost night. She wondered for a moment where she was going to sleep, but then she shook the thought away. She would find somewhere. She pushed the terrified whisper of the wolf to the back of her mind and went on. 'What was I doing here?'

'Exactly what I asked at the time,' the old swan muttered. 'It was the flood tide – it scoured all along the river. The rain had been going on for weeks, even worse than it is now, and there must have been some blockage further upstream, since it suddenly swept down all at once. I –' he hesitated, and Silken wondered if he was telling her all the truth of his story – 'I left my nest and went further in, to higher ground.' He snaked his long neck towards the birches, gesturing inland. 'When I came back the river was full of stinking mud and rubbish. Bodies too. Rats, mice. A fox.' He eyed Silken. 'That's what I thought you were. A body washed up in my nest. You weren't moving, just a soggy little ball of fur.'

The swan nibbled at his feathers again. 'I'd scraped a hole in the mud for the young fox,' he went on heavily. 'So I picked you up, and I meant to put you there too.' He looked up at her, his eyes hard and black. 'I was angry. I'd nested here for so long, and now I was going to have to move.'

'Because – because you can't have death in a nest?' Silken asked uncertainly.

'The nest was defiled,' he agreed. 'Nests are for eggs. For children. Not for a dead thing.'

As far as Silken knew, the old swan had no mate, and so there was no chance of the nest having eggs in, but she wasn't going to argue with him about it.

'I picked you up, and then you moved.' The swan glared at her, and Silken wondered if he expected her to apologise. It certainly seemed to be a distasteful memory. 'You wriggled and coughed, and spat up river water. You were alive. But you were tiny. You wouldn't have made it on your own.' He shifted uncomfortably. 'I didn't know what to do with you. I couldn't keep you and . . . well, you had fur. So I took you to the nearest furred creatures I knew.'

'The beavers . . .' Silken whispered.

'Your father was out inspecting the dam,' the swan explained. 'I gave you to him.'

'Did he think I was a beaver?' Silken asked. 'Did *he* think that I belonged?'

The swan gazed at her silently for a moment. 'I don't

know,' he admitted. 'I suppose even at that size, he must have known that you weren't from his own lodge. They had no kits missing. Perhaps he could see that you were not like others of his kind. But he took you in anyway. He must have felt it was his duty, to take care of a foundling.' He watched her silently for a moment, and then added, 'Or perhaps he needed you as much as you needed him.'

Silken looked away across the river. She couldn't think about her father's loneliness now. His kindness. He could have said no, that she wasn't one of their clan. He could have sent the old swan away. Silken suspected that if he had, she would not have lasted long. 'I wonder what he said to the others at the lodge,' she said, almost to herself. 'I suppose my mother must have agreed to take me.'

'I expect he told them all that you were an orphan of the storm, and they rallied around. He had no kits of his own, Master Grey, I remember that. It was a sadness to him. He must have hoped that you would grow up looking more like the rest of them.' He looked her up and down, and sighed. 'I suppose I should have taken you upstream instead. I did suspect that you weren't a beaver. But I had dealings with the lodge, they were familiar. I'd never spoken to an otter. Never met one.'

'Except for me,' Silken said quietly.

CHAPTER EIGHT

A nest, upriver

'It's coming on to rain again,' the old swan told Silken. He glanced into the darkness between the trees. 'You should get back to the lodge before it's full dark.'

Silken nodded. She could tell that he was eager to be rid of her. He wanted his quiet, peaceful nest back again.

'Yes, I'll go,' she said.

The swan's eyes glittered suspiciously. 'Where?' he asked.

'I don't think I can go back to the lodge. It doesn't feel like home any more. There were . . . the others *looked* at me . . . things were said, and now I know why. I never belonged there.'

'But what about your father?' the swan demanded, twisting his neck from side to side, as though he was in pain.

'He *isn't* my father,' Silken said stubbornly.

'He has tried to be!' The swan lowered his head to stare directly into Silken's eyes.

'There are those who care for you at the beaver lodge. Your father. Elders who have seen you grow up. And do you not have friends? Companions?'

Silken made a small squeak of agreement.

'You see! If you set off on your own you will have nothing,' he told her fiercely. 'Nothing and no one!'

'You can't know that,' she whispered. 'I might find my real family.'

'You might not.' The swan's voice was bleak, and he turned away from her.

'I feel alone at the lodge even now,' Silken tried to explain. She squashed down the few sweet memories of her quiet, reserved father. The clever toys he had made her. Standing next to him on top of the dam – she had felt she belonged then. She had been so proud that he had made something so special and that *she* was his daughter.

'You don't know what it is to be truly alone,' the swan whispered, his words hissing through the dark. 'It isn't brave, or clever, or heroic to have no one.'

But you're all alone here, Silken wanted to say. *Why did you never look for a mate, if it's so terrible to be alone?*

'I had a mate once,' the swan said, as if he'd heard her thoughts. 'I lost her – the same day that I found you.'

'In the flood?' Silken frowned, puzzled. His mate must surely have been able to swim, or to fly up out of the way of the rising river.

'The flood wasn't just water,' the swan explained. 'The river was choked with debris – branches, whole trees even. Bodies. Coming towards us, so fast, like a great wave. We'd never seen anything like it. A branch swirled past and tumbled out of the tide and hit my mate. It knocked her into the water.' His voice thinned. 'She was dead at once, I think. The river took her – as it must have taken you.'

'I'm sorry,' Silken whispered. 'I never knew.'

'I looked for her everywhere. Downstream. In along the banks. There was no sign of her – and then I came back, and I found you, half dead in her nest.' The swan uncoiled himself, and stood. 'It's too late even to start back to the lodge. There are rumours of the old wolf hunting along the river again, now that the water's high. You can't go anywhere now, otter cub.'

Otter cub – he meant *her*. The swan was no more than a faint pale shape in the darkness, and the river was shining black. There was an eerie silence all around – the creatures of the river and the bank had hidden themselves away. 'I'll find a space in the reeds,' she murmured. 'I can leave at first light.'

The swan made an irritable sort of noise, and stamped his feet. 'You've spent the night in this nest before. You may as well do it again.'

'Thank you,' Silken told him. She hadn't expected him to be so generous, even if he did look surly about it. She hesitated on the edge of the nest, not wanting to be too familiar. It wouldn't be right, to stomp in and settle herself down in the middle. She watched the swan curl himself around, tucking his beak underneath his wing. She tried to lie tight up against the side of the nest so that she didn't touch the old swan, but it was hard, when she was so tired. She could feel herself slumping sideways, nestling sleepily against the crisp feathers. As her eyes closed she felt his wing drop over her, and she sighed softly in the warmth.

She was in the water.

Not her beautiful river, warm and welcoming and full of eddies and ripples and cool dark patches, but something else. This water was a torrent. It took her and tumbled her, over and over, and Silken felt herself dashed against the river bed.

She thought she saw another dark shape go twisting by, just as desperate as she was, spluttering-crying, and turned every which way in the flood. Silken reached out, and their paws touched for a moment. Then the paw was torn away, and her tiny claws, reaching out in terror, grabbed only water. The other creature was gone, leaving only a faint whisper of a scream.

She was so tired. She ached.

Silken sighed, and let go . . .

'Here, stop that. Wake up.'

Silken whimpered, and then blinked awake, peering around in the early morning light.

The swan was staring at her, his head close down to hers.

'You were flailing about, squealing and crying. I thought we were being attacked! You had me ready to fight off a wolf! What's wrong with you?'

'I – I think it was a dream,' Silken murmured. 'I'm sorry.' The dream was still all around her – she was half out there in the river somewhere. She stretched her paws out, sure that she could still feel the bruises from that wild, battering ride through the water. She licked miserably at the fur on her chest. 'I was drowning.'

'A dream . . .' The swan ruffled up his feathers and looked at her thoughtfully. 'Are you sure it was a dream?'

'Of course it was! I was asleep, wasn't I? I have it sometimes, when it's raining.' Silken looked distastefully at the dripping trees. The swan's nest was so open, compared to the lodge. Even tucked under his wing, she had been rained on, and the nest felt damp and chilly.

When she'd dreamed the dream back at home – *not* home, back at the lodge, she corrected herself swiftly – her father had always come padding softly in to rescue her, dragging her up out of the waters of sleep, and telling her over and over that it was only a dream. He would sit with her, gently patting her paws until she felt safe to go to sleep again. She had forgotten that.

'What I meant was, perhaps it isn't *only* a dream.' The swan's eyes glinted. 'It could also be a memory. Since you did once almost drown.'

'Oh . . .' Silken whispered. 'I suppose I did remember then, after all.'

'Part of you remembered, deep inside,' the swan agreed. 'You were very small, it isn't surprising that you wanted to forget the flood. I would have forgotten, if I could.' He flinched, and the small feathers on his neck ruffled up.

'It wasn't like my river,' Silken burst out. 'The water was angry. It was cruel!'

'Yes,' the swan said. 'It was cruel.'

'Do you think I was swept away from that place – Greenwater?'

'Greenriver. The otter holt. It's a long way upstream. Too far for you to go.' But he sounded less definite about that than he had before.

'They're a settled holt, not like the band you must have seen passing through. The raft otters live by trade, as far as I know. They journey all the way down the river to the sea.'

'The sea!' Silken couldn't even imagine how far it was to the sea – or what the sea was like. Her father had tried to explain it once. A river that stretched on and on for ever, wider than you could see.

'I don't remember a holt,' she said, staring down at her paws, her eyes narrowed with the effort of remembering and not remembering. 'Only the flood, in my dream.' And perhaps someone reaching out for me. It doesn't seem fair, for that to be all I remember.'

The swan grunted. 'Is it so strange? Maybe you hit your head, when you were turned over and over in the water. Or maybe the water simply washed everything out of your skull.'

'Are you laughing at me?' Silken asked.

'Only a little.' He glanced away, out to the water. 'So. I suppose now you want to go upstream to Greenriver.'

Silken looked at him in surprise. 'Last night you said it wasn't safe, and it was best to stay with what I knew.'

'I still think that. But . . . if the flood is haunting your dreams – well, dreams are important. Dreams have meaning.'

Silken looked out at the river. It should have been encouraging, to be told to set out on the journey she wanted. But the energy had gone out of her. She felt lost and tired and weak. And there was a wolf out there, on the hunt. The wolf seemed a lot less of a legend, now that she was about to head upriver alone.

'It's a long way,' the old swan told her, as if he could sense her doubts. 'You could go back to the lodge now. Go home and forget this happened.'

'It isn't my home,' Silken said, shaking her head. 'But I do have to go back first. You were right when you said my father tried his best. It would be cruel to leave him, without some sort of message.'

'You've already been missing a night,' the swan pointed out. 'They'll be out looking for you soon, I'd say. When the sun's properly up.'

She nodded, though inside, she was wondering if many of the beavers *would* be out looking. What if they were relieved that she had gone? *Speckle and Frost would miss me*, she told herself. And her father. 'He won't let me set off upriver on my own,' she said. 'I'll have to sneak back in, so as not to be seen.'

The sun was nearly fully risen. If she was going back to leave her message, it would have to be now.

Silken turned back to bow politely to the swan. 'It's getting light. I'll miss my chance if I don't go now. Thank you, for the night's shelter, and the talk. And for your kindness to mc all that time ago, after the flood.'

He nodded back. 'Safe travels. I hope you find what you're searching for.'

There was nothing left to say. Silken slipped over the edge of the reed nest and into the water. It was pinkish with reflected light from the sky, and she swam through a thin mist rising off the river. It was very quiet, and the mist muffled the faint sound of her splashing even more. She felt invisible, sneaking down the river like the little spy the swan had accused her of being.

The mist was not going to help her get into the lodge though. The lodge could only be reached by swimming underwater – there were no back doors, or secret entrances.

And if she swam through the tunnel, she would be seen. Someone was always watching the entrance. There was nothing quite as official as a guard duty, just – always someone there. One of the old ones weaving a bag, perhaps, or snoozing on a log against the wall. As soon as she entered the tunnel, the lodge would know that Master Grey's difficult daughter was back.

Silken drew into the far bank as she came up to the lodge, keeping an eye out for early risers. She couldn't see anyone out in the water. There was certainly no anxious search party calling her name.

She skirted past the lodge itself to the dam. Her father would be out for his early morning inspection soon. If she could anchor a message somewhere along the top of the dam, he would be sure to see it.

But what could she write her message on? She peered along the dam, looking for a likely bit of timber. The morning light was settling now, the wild colours of the sky fading to a clear blue, but there was still an amber gleam on the water – and on a piece of silver birch half buried inside the dam, the pale bark already peeling off in curls. Silken tugged off a strip. She had no soot and gall ink, or even a charred stick to write with, but a scrape with a claw would do.

What was she to say though?

At last she scratched, *Gone upriver to find the otters. Thank you.*

It was not enough, not near enough. But what else could she say?

Searching around, she pulled a forked stick out of the mass of twigs and branches, and stuck it upright into the tangle. Then she slotted her message inside the fork, and sighed. It looked secure. He would find it, she hoped. It was the best she could do.

Then she scurried back along the dam, and slid into the water again. She was swimming upriver, and she didn't know if she would ever come back down.

CHAPTER NINE

On the river, a night's swim
downstream from the Holt

Sedge had been out on the river at night before – night swimming had been an important part of his education. But he had rarely swum on his own in the dark. As he crept out of the holt's back door and slipped into the river, the water closed over him like the softest black fur. He could feel the silky cold of it seeping into his coat as he swam downriver, keeping under the surface as long as he could, in case an otter from the holt should be out night-fishing and catch a glimpse of him.

He surfaced to breathe only among the reeds, or beneath overhanging banks, darting his head up like a conspirator. The excitement bubbled inside him, and every so often his teeth showed in a wild grin. He was away!

It was hard to tell how long he had been swimming without the sun to watch, but when he felt too tired to keep going, he climbed out on to the bank. The night cold was slowing him and his limbs felt heavy and thick, as if he were swimming through soup.

Sedge sniffed carefully, trying to tell if there were other creatures anywhere close. Rabbits, he thought. Maybe a water vole. No one big enough to be a threat – and there was no rank scent of wolf. He shook himself thoroughly, his fur sticking up in a thousand little arrows. Then he dropped to the ground, flattening a patch of long grass as he rolled and wriggled back and forth, squeezing the water out of his fur.

He was starting to feel a little warmer now, and he yawned, sleepy. He combed through his fur with his claws as quickly as he could, drying off his coat and oiling up the hairs to keep himself waterproof. It was an effort to twist and reach and comb all along his back, but if he didn't do it, his coat would be sodden and freezing as soon as he dived into the river the next morning.

At last, grooming done, Sedge padded further inland, snuffling around among the tree roots for a hole to huddle up in. Now that he was no longer swimming, it felt dangerous to be out in the open at night. The shadows around him seemed full of whispers, and he thought once he heard the thud of heavy paws. He wondered if anyone had noticed that he'd gone.

He almost blundered into the tree, its long branches curving down towards the ground like steps. Sedge gazed up at it, dopey with weariness, and considered. Teasel would snort in disgust at the idea of him sleeping in a tree. Otters slept in holts, or at worst, in a temporary hover in a clump of bracken, or a hollow under tree roots. Trees were for birds. Or squirrels.

But he was alone and vulnerable and the tree looked welcoming. When he patted one paw cautiously against a branch, he found that it was soft with velvet moss. Sedge padded up on to it, weaving his way through the green-gold leaves, and followed it back to where it joined the trunk. From his lessons with the healers at the holt, he thought the tree was a sycamore, though it was hard to tell in the dark.

He curled up, nestled in the cushiony moss, and lay listening to the night noises all around. The river chattered on as a quiet background to rustling and footsteps and the calls of night birds. Sedge felt small and lonely up in the tree. But he was on a quest, he reminded himself sleepily. He was going to find his sister and bring her back and be a hero. How could he be scared?

The fear had eased by the next morning. It was damp and mizzling again, chilly for late spring, but at least there was light. Sedge bounded down the branch and into the water, hunting for breakfast. He was able to snap up a few small roach, their reddish fins and tails flickering away through the dull water as he shot after them. After eating, he brushed the scales from his fur with fastidious paws, and sucked his teeth. Time to travel on.

Now that it was daylight, he could hunt for news of Elderberry, for the birds who had passed her song on up the river. The last Dark Spring was recent enough that creatures all along the riverbank would remember it, he was sure. Someone must have heard of a young otter, washed up after the great flood. There would be stories and rumours and fragments of gossip, and eventually, surely, he would find some real news. As long as he started back upriver no later than a day or two after the moon turned, he would be back before his mother's new ritual. There was plenty of time, perhaps ten days or so, though he would have to watch the moon.

The rising water levels over the last few seasons must have changed the shape of the river, Sedge thought, eyeing the deeply undercut bank opposite him, and trying to remember his lessons with Teasel. There had always been known spots for scavenging finds from the river, where anything that had been swept along by the current washed up. Teasel had told him of another old willow tree, a day's journey downriver from the holt, that caught treasures in its trailing roots.

When Elderberry had been flooded out of the holt, she would have been swept on downstream until there was some sort of obstruction. That old willow tree maybe, or somewhere else the river channel narrowed. Rapids, or a waterfall. He would look for something like that and ask any creature he passed along the way.

It seemed very little to go on.

You're having an adventure, Sedge told himself stoutly as he swam on down the middle of the wide river. He was far enough from the holt not to sneak and sidle now, he reckoned, even though it was full daylight. Greenriver otters hardly ever came this far downstream.

A few bends of the river later, round mid-morning, he spotted the fine yellow-green fronds of a willow tree and sped up, cutting eagerly through the water. Was this the tree Teasel had spoken of? His teacher had described the roots, trailing into the river, but not like this. Sedge circled the tree, peering into the lacy branches. The tree was *in* the river – its great trunk torn away from the bank entirely, the roots sticking up in the air in a strange fur-like tangle.

The willow was huge, and yet the river had sucked away the earth around it, and plunged it into the water. The fall had been recent, Sedge thought, clambering out on to the bank and sniffing at the great gouges torn in the mud. This spring. Sedge watched the water foaming as it rushed in and out of the sodden branches, and shivered.

There were sticks and weeds caught in the willow branches, already building up into fat clumps. Last spring the roots must have been like a net, reaching deep into the water, just right for clawing a tiny otter cub out of the flood. Elderberry could have ended up here.

Sedge sniffed the air. There were creatures around, he could tell, but they were all considerably smaller than he was, and they were clearly hiding. When a large stranger arrived in their territory, it was only sensible to go to ground.

'Er, is anyone here?' he tried hopefully. 'Could I talk to you? I'm looking for someone.'

No answer, just that odd, listening silence. A faint shuffling of feathers in the trees – apart from that, not even a chirruping. But he could smell other creatures, their scent on the grass and the bracken under the trees.

Sedge sighed. 'I'm just going to rest here for a bit. All right?' He crept a little way from the water, and stamped round and round in the bracken, squashing the stems down to make a resting place.

He was being watched. The eyes prickled over his fur and he wriggled uncomfortably on his bracken bed. In the end, he stood up, glaring round at the invisible watchers. 'I only wanted a place to sleep,' he growled. 'Riverbank doesn't belong to you,' he added, conveniently forgetting that the holt guarded their section of the river too.

The hush deepened, and even the noise of the water seemed to die away – and then Sedge heard a sharp crack, as a fallen branch snapped under a heavy paw. He felt the fur rise up all along his spine as he realised. It wasn't *him* that everyone was hiding from.

Sedge froze, ready to run. Was he hidden well enough among the bracken? And – what was it? Deep down, he already knew, but the creature stalking along the riverbank still stole the breath out of his chest.

A wolf. The hugest animal that Sedge had ever seen. She was old, with thin, patchy grey fur stretched over her bones, but her paws were still the size of Sedge's skull. She lifted her head, weaving as she snuffed the air, and yellow teeth showed at the edge of her mouth like knives.

Something deep inside Sedge, some ancient instinct, was telling him to go, go now and race away down the bank, but he resisted. She hadn't seen him, but she would, as soon as he moved.

Instead, he crouched shivering among the bracken stems, trying not to breathe as the wolf passed by, hoping that the bracken was masking his scent. The yellow-green stems shivered as her heavy paws thudded by his hiding place – and then she stopped, close enough that Sedge could see the pale cast over her eye. She had to have seen him. But then she shambled on, heading downstream along the bank. Sedge watched her, peering through the bracken, and realised that her pale eye was blind. If he had chosen the clump of bracken on the other side of her path . . .

It took a long time for him to breathe properly again.

He had heard so many stories, but he had never expected to see the night wolf for himself. It had been hard to believe that she really existed. No creature could be that big, that dangerous. No creature could have lived that long! She was a story, an old legend and that was all. But now the legend was real. And he had to follow her down the river.

Even after the wolf had gone, the riverbank stayed still and silent. Sedge slipped into the water and swam on, staying out in the deep central channel of the river. He kept to the

water as much as he could from then on, hardly daring to set paw on the riverbank. He swam much longer distances than he was used to, stopping only when he spotted places the river had been casting up its finds, and he hoped to find some news of Elderberry. His sleeps were short, and uneasy, and he began to hate being so alone. He missed Lily and Tormentil and the others so much. He'd almost have been glad to see Pebble.

Were they missing him? No one knew where he had gone – for all they knew, the old wolf *had* swallowed him down. His mother would think she'd lost another cub. But if there was even a chance that he could bring Elderberry back, he was sure that all this would be worth it. Almost sure.

Some nights into his journey, Sedge was crouched on a flat expanse of shingle where the river widened, tearing into a fat trout and listening, as always, for the heavy pad of paws. There were birds calling in the trees further back up the bank, close enough for him to catch their sharp chattering.

'An otter, do you see?'

'Is that what it is?'

'Do they hunt birds?'

'My eggs!'

'No, no . . . Look. Just fish. Great ugly thing.'

Sedge hunched up over the trout, and the delicious mouthful seemed to catch in his throat. Birds. Silly twittery mites. What did he care what they thought? Still, after all those silent, frightened days in the wake of the night wolf, it was comforting to hear voices, even if they were calling him ugly. He straightened a little, and then slowly stood up on his hindquarters, listening hard.

The birds hushed for a moment, and then one of them murmured again:

'Does it hear us?'

'It's listening!'

'Scatter!'

'No! No!' Sedge pleaded, scuttling over the shingle towards the trees. 'Listen, please! I only want to ask you . . .'

But he could hear the rustle of frantic wings as they fled – and then it was back to that strange dead quiet, the only sound the water rushing on and on. Sedge had never thought he'd be tired of hearing his beloved river.

A day or so more, he promised himself. Just a little further. The moon was rising up above the empty trees now, a thin pale crescent in the sky. He hadn't long before it began to grow and swell again, back to the full moon – and the ceremony his mother and the holt were depending on.

If there was no news of Elderberry soon, he would have

to accept it and turn back so as to be home in time. Sedge dreaded giving up on his sister, but a tiny part of him, one that he hated but couldn't deny, was desperate to swim back upriver as fast as he could, so he could stay out of the way of the wolf.

He would have to slink back into the holt, though, and explain where he had been. He'd have to admit that he had been off on a wild goose chase, haring after a childish dream. When he'd heard Lily and Tormentil singing Elderberry's song it had seemed so real. Their voices had swept him away in a tide of hope. Out here on his own though, it all felt empty.

Sedge sent the bones of the trout spinning out into the shallow waters with an angry sweep of his paw. How could he leave his sister out here, if there was even the tiniest chance that she was still alive?

Just a little further on.

***

It was his final day, the day he had told himself must be his very last going downriver. Sedge was up with the dawn, watching pinkish-orange light flood across the sky. Mist was rising off the river, and the morning was chilly.

Sedge shuddered a little as he slipped into the water, feeling the cold seep in as far as his underfur. He would find someone to speak to today, he told himself. He must. He would find news of Elderberry – or he would give up and go home.

When the sun was fully risen and warming the fur across the top of his head, Sedge began to look around for a hopeful place to stop. Somewhere that looked as if it might be busy, where he could ask about Elderberry. He kept a careful eye out for tracks, or pellets, or scat, but it seemed the river had washed all the signs away.

Then he rounded a sweeping bend and saw a sandy bank, full of little holes, and scurrying paths leading up into the grass on the higher ground above. *Water voles.* Lots of them, it looked like. Surely at least one would talk to him? Sedge found his heart racing just at the thought of company, even if they had no news of his sister.

He swam swiftly to the edge of the water and bundled out on to a patch of sticky mud between the roots. Then he popped up on to the short, nibbled grass and practically fell into a marketplace.

Between two great twisted roots of an oak tree a crowd of tiny voles, mice and shrews had set out their wares. Neat woven grass mats were covered in berries, dried herbs, and acorn cups polished to a shining smoothness. Sedge looked down and saw that his left front paw was now covered in what had probably been bilberry jam, and a plump wood mouse was staring in horror at her crushed jars.

'Oh! Oh, I'm sorry . . .' He tried to retreat, feeling bigger and clumsier than he had ever felt before, but every paw seemed to be about to squash something – or someone. He sucked in his breath and tried to tiptoe backwards on the points of his claws, while all around him shrews gathered their panicked, squeaking babies, and harvest mice hustled away down tiny paths through the grasses.

Before he'd managed to retreat to the path down the bank, the entire marketplace was empty. Only the woven mats and the spilled market goods were left. There was no one to ask for news of his sister. He was never going to be able to find her.

Sedge slunk miserably back to the water. It was no good. He would have to go home and explain, and resign himself to being a bad, clumsy lord of the holt. He would hunt first, to give him the energy he needed for the long swim back, and then he'd start the journey upstream.

A short while later, he was crouched on a mudflat, a little further down from the ruined mouse market, spitting bones out of a lucky catch – a young pike that must have been daydreaming. Pike were tricky prey, usually, but this one had swum right under his nose. He was tearing into it so savagely that he didn't notice the bird sitting above him on a trailing willow branch at all.

'Good eating?'

Sedge jumped and whirled round to show his teeth at the speaker.

'What do you want?'

'I'm not trying to take it off you, youngster,' the kingfisher trilled. 'Though of course if you had any spare, I'd not say no. Plenty of meat on a pike, and it's not something I'd be able to catch myself.'

Sedge peered up at the bird, breathing a little more easily now that the surprise had worn off. 'You're welcome to some. More than I can eat, and I'm travelling. I can't cache it anywhere.'

'Thank you kindly. You couldn't bite me off a piece, could you? I catch everything whole, you see. Don't have the right sort of beak for tearing.'

Sedge bit off a piece of fish near the tail and dropped it under the bird's branch. Then he hopped back in surprise as it darted by in a shining flash of blue and snatched the food before it had even hit the ground.

'Very good. Very good indeed,' the kingfisher muttered thickly above him. 'Thank you.'

Sedge felt the misery inside him ease a little, softened by the friendly words. 'Would you answer me a question?' he asked, between mouthfuls. 'You can have some more of this, if you want.'

'Go on then.' The kingfisher fluttered its wings, ready to dive again, and this time Sedge tossed the fish into the air for it to catch.

'Did you ever see any other otters on this part of the river?'

The kingfisher gulped hard and fluffed out its orange belly feathers. 'Only the traders on the raft. They pass by.'

'Oh.' Sedge crunched bones thoughtfully. He knew of the raft otters, of course. His father's people. They always stopped at the holt out of courtesy and brought gifts for his mother.

'Why are you asking?' the kingfisher asked, with a meaningful glance at the pike. Sedge slung another piece into the air, and the kingfisher arrowed towards it, then huddled smugly back on the branch, looking full.

'I am searching for my sister.' Last night the moon had been only a sliver in the sky. He had been away for the whole of the moon's waning – and he had to return. If he was going back – and he *must* go back for the ceremony, or risk the waters rising even further and endangering the holt – he had to go now.

In all that time, he had not spoken to anyone who had seen Elderberry. He had hardly spoken to anyone at all. His quest – such a grand word – was feeling more and more like a silly pup's foolish idea. Elderberry herself seemed further away than ever.

'I ran away from the holt to try and find her,' he explained. 'She was washed out of our holt by the flood at the Dark Spring. Uh, do you call it that? We otters call it the Dark Spring, when the river rises so high . . .'

'Everyone calls it that,' the kingfisher agreed, peering down at him curiously. 'Excuse me asking this, but don't otters swim? What harm did it do her, the river flooding?'

'We hadn't yet learned to swim,' Sedge murmured. 'We were too small. I was rescued, but no one ever found Elderberry. Not even – not even her body. So I came to look for her. I heard her song . . .'

'She sings?' The bird cocked its head sideways.

'She did. All otters sing.' Sedge thought the kingfisher looked doubtful about this, but he hurried on. 'But the song I heard was her own song, one she made for us, out of our names. No one else ever sang it, only her and me, before she was lost . . . and then I heard it again. Just days ago.' Sedge stared down at his claws. 'Two of my friends were singing it – they'd picked it up from a flock of willow warblers, in the reeds close to our holt. That's when I knew she must still be alive, downriver somewhere. She's been singing our song, and now it's travelled back up the river.'

'Mmm.' The bird considered. 'Are you sure? More likely the warblers heard your sister sing it when she was small, seems to me. You just never noticed them before now. Great tall creatures like you, you don't see us birds.'

Sedge stared at him, aghast. 'Don't say that,' he whispered. 'Please. Even if I can't find her, the song means Elderberry's still alive. It does.'

'Elderberry?' The kingfisher poked his head forward. 'Ah! Now, that's a song I know!' He chirped harshly, clearing his throat, and then sang, *'Ripe black elderberries, gleaming in the sun . . .'* in a cracked little voice. 'Up and down the riverbank like wildfire, that one's gone. That your sister's song?'

Sedge nodded. There were too many words jammed up in his throat to speak. 'No one will talk to me. They run away when I try.'

'Is it any wonder?' the kingfisher trilled sharply, and Sedge realised that it found him funny. 'Did you not hear that the wolf is out on the riverbank? *Everyone's* hiding. Besides, even if it weren't for the wolf, you otters, you keep yourselves to yourselves. You never talk. You see another riverbank creature and you show your teeth and then half a dozen other otters pop up. Everyone else knows not to mess with you.'

'Oh.' Sedge hadn't thought of it like that. But he supposed it was true – he had only seen it from the other side. He would call it the otters protecting their own.

'Very curious, I was, to see a haughty holt otter all alone,' the kingfisher went on. 'But since you've been kind enough to share your fish, I'll tell you something in exchange.'

'You *have* seen her?' Sedge squeaked hopefully. 'You heard her singing?'

'No.' The kingfisher hopped down to a lower branch, closer to Sedge. 'No, I'm sorry. But I know who you should ask. You go on down the river, perhaps a day's flight more, and find the old swan. He has a nest in the reeds under a gathering of silver birch trees. You ask him. Everyone knows him, and he knows everything that happens along the river. He'll know where that song started.' The kingfisher hesitated and seemed unsure whether to go on.

'What?' Sedge turned his paws over and over each other, without even realising that he was at it.

'He lost his mate in the flood. He may not want to talk about the dark days.'

But Sedge was already scurrying eagerly towards the water. 'Thank you!' he called back. 'If I find her, we'll come back this way! I'll bring her to meet you!'

The kingfisher watched as the small otter flung himself into the river and paddled away, only his head and base of his long, rudder-like tail showing above the silver-grey water. 'Good hunting, youngster,' he muttered.

The otter was out of sight by the time the ripples had faded.

CHAPTER TEN

On the river, between the
Holt and the Lodge

Sedge swam on long into the night, stopping only for the shortest of preenings. He had to get back up the river to the holt in time for his mother's new ceremony – he had promised himself that the waxing moon would see him turn back, but he couldn't ignore what the kingfisher had told him.

Sedge's muscles were screaming at him for rest, but he kept going. By the time the moon rose that night, a thin hooked claw, he was exhausted. He hadn't yet come to the grove of birches that the kingfisher had described, but he knew he could go no further without a rest.

Sedge paddled closer to the bank, looking for a place to sleep. Somewhere sheltered. He hoped that he had been moving downstream faster than the wolf could have followed, but he didn't want to leave that to chance. He needed a hole under a root, or a hollow tree, not just a patch of flattened bracken. He was so tired that he might miss the signs of a threat approaching – he needed to be safely tucked away.

In the faint moonlight, the matted little pile of sticks looked like a swan's nest for a moment. Sedge's heart leaped – had he found the old swan after all? But then he saw that the trees were a tangle of ash and willow saplings, not silver birches, and he realised that the sticks were a strange sort of shelter, a lean-to built up against the largest ash tree.

One of his lessons with Teasel had been about the building habits of beavers. She had freely admitted that she had never seen a beaver – who would want to? – but Sedge had found the lesson fascinating anyway. How grand, to alter the whole course of Lady River with one's building!

Teasel had been very sniffy about it, calling the process *unnatural*. Lady River should flow where she wanted, and it was sacrilege to try to change her ways. Sedge didn't see that it was any different from their rituals, though, and perhaps in some ways, it was better. Otters only prayed for Lady River not to flood; beavers actually did something about it. But of course, he'd never said that to anyone.

One of the things Teasel had told him – disapprovingly – was that beaver dams and lodges were just messy piles of sticks, even worse than birds' nests. And that was what this strange little house looked like, more than anything. A huge, untidy nest.

It also looked warm, dry and comfortable.

Cautiously, Sedge nosed out of the water, and crept towards the dark opening. Something so snug and cosy probably already had an owner, fast asleep inside. He sniffed hopefully around the doorway. It smelled . . . pleasant. More pleasant than he had expected, given that it had probably been built by a beaver.

Sedge crept a little way into the house, out of the wind, and shivered happily. It was the middle of the night, and this snug den was empty.

There was a big pile of dry leaves in one corner, the most comfortable bed Sedge had seen in a long time. Had Teasel said that beavers hunted at night? He couldn't remember. But it didn't matter, his tired brain pointed out hopefully. If the beaver was out hunting, Sedge could borrow its bed, just for a little while. No reason to leave such a good bed empty. Besides, he could be out of the den in moments, and safely hidden in the trees, as soon as he heard someone. He was sure he'd hear the beaver coming back.

He didn't.

Not in time, anyway. By the time he woke, there was already a faint padding of paws at the doorway. Sedge surged up out of the pile of leaves still half asleep. He grabbed at the hilt of his belt knife, feeling it stick a little as he drew it out, and wished that he'd been better about cleaning and polishing it to guard against the river-damp.

Sedge bared his teeth and narrowed his eyes, peering across the tiny space. Hardly any moonlight was coming in, just the faintest gleam around the shoulders of the dark creature in the doorway. His heart thumped, half expecting the night wolf to shake the little den down around them, but then he realised what he was seeing, and worked out that this creature was the same size that he was. The beaver then? Back to claim its den? Sedge took a firmer grip on the hilt of his knife, and waited.

The beaver waited too. The pair of them stared at each other uncertainly.

'This is my lodge,' the beaver said at last. She – Sedge was almost sure she was a female – sounded not much older than he was. And she most definitely wasn't a wolf. Sedge managed to take a full breath for the first time since he'd woken up.

'I'm a traveller,' he explained, lowering the knife a little. 'I was looking for a place to shelter, that's all. I thought this den was empty. I mean, it *was* empty. Oh . . . you know what I mean. I'll go. If you let me.'

'Go then.' She stepped away from the door, but he could feel her waiting. He wondered if she was armed at all. She sounded fierce.

Sedge kicked away the leaves around his paws, and tried to walk out with dignity, not like a cub who'd been caught napping in someone else's den. As he came out of the doorway, he glanced sideways, curious to see what a beaver really looked like.

She was standing on her back paws, hunched over and squat, but otherwise she was surprisingly like an otter. Sedge had expected something very different. He stopped, and peered at her more closely, squinting in the clouded moonlight.

She was trembling.

Sedge was torn, half guilty that he had frightened her, and half triumphant. A beaver was afraid of him! He was actually frightening! After the days of travelling in constant fear, it was horribly good to frighten someone else. Then the thump of his heart slowed a little, and his guilt won out. He sheathed the knife and bowed to her – but not too low, and still keeping his paw on the hilt, just in case.

'I'm sorry to have trespassed on your hospitality.'

'It doesn't matter.' She straightened up a little, waving her paw as if to hurry him on.

At that moment, the scurrying clouds swept over the narrow moon and away, and the two creatures saw each other properly for the first time.

'You aren't a beaver!' Sedge yelped, as Silken gasped, 'An otter!'

Sedge let go of his knife and stepped nearer to the strange otter, peering at her in the half-light of the moon. He reached out one paw, and for a moment she reached out to him too. But then she quickly snatched her paw back, and stared at him in confusion.

The other otter stood so hunched over that it was hard to tell, but she seemed to be about the same size as Sedge was – and the same age. Her fur was dark, with a reddish tinge that reminded him of elderberries . . .

Sedge swallowed hard, wishing away the dark. Everything in him had been fighting to reach the old swan, to find news of his sister – and now . . . could it be? He felt as if he'd been caught in a current, spun over and round so that he was dizzy, and blinking. Could it really be her? Sedge scanned her hungrily, wishing that his night sight was a little stronger . . . there was hardly any light . . . but he knew those eyes. The way the pale fur under her chin shone against her berry-dark coat. He knew that too. They had curled up together as tiny cubs, his head tucked under that chin.

Sedge gasped in a breath, feeling a wild joy bubble up inside him, pouring through him like wild water.

'What . . . who are you?' she whispered. She shook her head, as if she was trying to shake her thoughts clear.

'I found you!' Sedge gasped at the same time. 'I found you, I found you, I found you!' He was dancing from paw to paw. He wanted to grab her and swing her round and round, but there wasn't space in the tiny den – and she still looked terrified. More terrified than she had been when she thought he was some sort of thieving invader. Sedge swallowed hard, trying to catch and slow the joyful words that wanted to bubble out of him.

Very slowly, the strange, stooped, dark-furred otter stepped forward, and nudged noses with him, almost tangling their whiskers. Sedge could feel the uncertainty, and the longing, in that tiny moment.

But then she pulled back, gazing at him in bewilderment. 'Why do I know you?'

***

Silken watched the otter – the *other* otter. She was suddenly cold, and she could feel her heart thumping to the ends of her fur. He was a stranger, but she knew him. The scent of him,

the silvery moonlight gleam over his fur, seemed so familiar. It was as if she was straining to catch a thread of song, only half heard. The notes wouldn't stay . . .

A song. There was a song.

He stopped twirling and hopping and gazed back at her.

'You don't remember?' He looked lost now. Silken felt a strange instinct rising inside her, as if she ought to comfort him. She shook her head and watched him sag a little. He stood there, winding his paws over each other. 'I suppose I should have thought of that. Of course. I had forgotten too. And if you remembered, surely you'd have tried to come back.' He gazed at her helplessly. 'It's hard to know where to start . . .'

'Come back where?' Silken whispered.

'To our holt. Greenriver. It's upstream from here.'

Our holt?

The dark, deep water coldness wrapped itself even tighter around Silken. How could she not know? Who was this otter, this stranger who knew more about herself than she did, who said *our*? Who thought she belonged. It seemed so unbelievably cruel, that she belonged somewhere but she didn't know it, she couldn't feel it.

He stumbled on, the happiness draining out of his words. 'I came to find you. I heard your song, you see. The warblers were singing it. Before – when we were little – you only sang that song to me. It was ours, no one at the holt would sing it but us. I thought that hearing it again meant you were alive. You had to be alive.' He was silent for a moment, and then he added, in a smaller voice, 'I was right.' Then he closed his eyes – Silken watched them close, the glittering darkness disappear – and said in the smallest voice of all, 'You're my sister.'

It was everything that Sedge had wanted. Somehow though, when he'd imagined finding Elderberry, the details had been lost in a soft dawn-in-the-river-mist glow. She had hugged him, of course, and then they'd set off happily back to the holt. Where everyone greeted him as a hero, and his mother stopped grieving and sang to the river again.

He hadn't expected there to be so much explaining. He hadn't reckoned on Elderberry not even knowing who he was.

Calling her his sister seemed to have silenced her entirely. Sedge carried on in the brittle quiet. 'Your name's Elderberry. At least, that's what it was, when you were back at home.'

'My name is Silken,' she said. 'But I know the elderberry song.'

'*Ripe black elderberries . . .*' Sedge sang. He'd hoped she might join in, but all she did was nod.

'I sang that out on the riverbank,' she murmured. 'Just before . . .'

'Before what?' Sedge asked.

'Before I saw a gang of raft otters.' She sighed. 'They were singing, the way I do. No one else sang like that, not at the Stronghold.' She saw him frowning, and twitched at her tail. 'You don't understand! I'd always been scared of otters!'

'But . . . you *are* an otter,' Sedge said.

She hunched over again. 'Until a few days ago, I thought I was a beaver. I mean, I *knew* I was a beaver, I didn't think about it at all, I just was! But then I saw those raft otters.'

'I've never seen a beaver,' Sedge admitted. 'But I thought they were very different from us.' He could hear the distaste in his voice, the fear, even. He couldn't help it. He had been brought up to think that beavers were everything that otters were not. It wasn't helping him to be tactful now.

'They are. But I just thought I was skinny, and . . . wrong. I was no good at all the things the others my age could do, and I couldn't stop singing.'

'That's what I remember most about you,' he told her shyly. 'You could sing stories. Even when we were little, the

157

others at the holt loved your stories. But you mostly sang them to me. Didn't the beavers like your singing?' he asked, feeling indignant.

'My friends did. They'd ask me to sing, sometimes. But the older beavers thought singing was strange – I got looks.'

Sedge nodded sympathetically.

'And my father didn't like it. I kept forgetting. Well. Not forgetting exactly. The songs just seemed to happen.'

'Your father?' Sedge stared at her in bewilderment.

'Oh . . .' She slumped down on the pile of leaves. 'I know he isn't. But I've called him that ever since I can remember.' Her whole body seemed to sigh, nose to tail. 'It slipped out, like the songs.'

Sedge settled next to her, carefully apart. 'He said that you were his own child? Why?'

'I don't know. I didn't ask him, I left. I did write a note.'

Sedge snorted. 'I didn't.'

'You mean, no one knows you're here either?'

Sedge hesitated, wondering if there was a way to explain without upsetting her again. 'They wouldn't have let me come,' he said gently. 'Everyone – everyone thinks that you're dead, you see.'

She curled her muzzle, and then said in a strange, flat voice, 'Did I drown?'

Sedge nodded. 'I couldn't save you.'

That brought her swinging round to stare at him. 'Of course not! How could you save me? You were a cub! Tiny!'

'Yes . . .' It was easier to hear that, when Elderberry herself said it. 'I'd had so many dreams about you, but I thought they were only dreams. I was starting to understand that I'd lost something, but I didn't really remember the flood or you – not until I heard your song. *Our* song. Then everything came back so clearly, it was like shaking water out of my ears . . .' He sighed. 'And I realised that everyone thought you were dead, but no one *knew*, not for certain.'

He frowned, trying to remember back to that moment on the riverbank. Then he said, 'I wanted to do something big. Something brave. Lily – she and Tormentil are my friends, it was them who first heard the warblers singing your song – she has a brother. Pebble. He's the biggest of all the cubs, he's the same age as me but he's huge, you'd think he had a summer on us. We had a fight. Except that makes it sound like I actually got a paw near, and I don't think I touched him. He almost drowned me.'

'Why?' she asked, her voice rising angrily.

Sedge's heart lightened a little at her sharpness. 'He's jealous, I suppose. Or he just doesn't like me. It made me want to show him that I'm not as useless as all that. I was going on a quest. To show everyone, not only Pebble.' He ducked his head, embarrassed.

'And you did it.'

'Yes . . .'

She shot him a cold-eyed glance. 'Do you wish you hadn't?'

'No! But I wanted it to be the same as it was before. I thought that you'd know who I was . . .'

His sister said nothing to that – there was nothing that either of them could say.

❦

Sedge lay awake for what felt like a long while, wondering about this odd, sharp-tongued creature. *This* was Elderberry? No otter would build a den like this! She was odd-looking too, huddled over like that. And she didn't understand anything about otters.

He had come searching for Elderberry, his beautiful, clever sister, and he hadn't found her. Instead he'd come upon a creature who built dens like a beaver, with strange hunched shoulders, and a waddling walk. She was an otter – but she wasn't. And he didn't *love* her.

In her corner, Silken worried at a dry leaf between

160

her paws. The first otter she had met, and she'd snarled at him. But he was such a silly, childish sort of thing. All that nervous twisting of his paws, and so horrified that she'd lived with beavers, and built herself a house of sticks! Why shouldn't she? He'd been glad enough to shelter in it when the rain started.

Silken wriggled herself deeper into the leaves, and stared at the dark. What if she didn't fit in any better at a holt than she had at a beaver lodge? She supposed there was nothing stopping her wandering on – and on. She shivered at the thought. She didn't want to be all on her own for ever. She had wanted a home. But now home had come looking for her, and she wasn't sure about it at all.

Eventually, both Sedge and Silken fell asleep, worn out by hard travel, loneliness and fear. They muttered and shivered among the leaves until the darkest part of the night, when the rain died down and the riverbank became eerily silent, and even the foxes sloped back to their beds. Then they both began to dream.

As the dream water came inching up the tunnel towards the cubs' sleeping chamber, Sedge and Silken rolled towards each other, nuzzling and wriggling like the babies they had been. Sedge nested his head under Silken's chin and caught the sweet river scent of her fur. His eyelids flickered, and he sighed.

Silken snuffled into his fur, mumbling to herself as the dream began to sweep her away, the dark water closing over her head. She flailed her paws as she tried to fight her way through the dream river, squeaking and choking and gobbling with fear. Then, just as the dark and cold rolled over her, she felt a paw catch in hers. Someone was trying to carry her back to the surface.

Sedge felt panicked paws scrabbling against his fur and whined. He stretched out, desperately reaching for his sister as the water tried to tear him away. Deep inside, he knew that it wouldn't work. He'd lose her again, as he had so many times.

But then their paws touched, and caught, and held.

The two otters sprang awake and blinked at each other in the faint moonlight.

'Did you dream . . .?' Silken whispered gruffly, and Sedge nodded at her.

'It's the same dream I always have,' he murmured. 'But I never hold on . . . I get rescued, pulled out of the water, and the other otter is gone.'

'In my dream no one ever reaches me. I touch a paw, that's all, but then it slips away. Except this time it didn't.' She stared at him. 'You really did try to save me.'

'You remember?' he asked her hopefully, his paw still on hers.

Silken thought about saying yes. She was so close to remembering. If she said yes, it would mean that she had a family. But the memory wasn't much of a memory at all. Just a tiny fragment, the dream she'd always had. She couldn't bring herself to lie to him, and to keep on lying.

She had been silent for a moment too long already. 'No,' she told him sadly. 'No, I don't.'

CHAPTER ELEVEN

On the river, between the
Lodge and the Holt

Sedge woke late the next morning. His sleep had been disturbed with dreams, and yet the bed of leaves was comfortable – every time he woke up, he huddled back into the pile again. He woke feeling slow and stupid and chilled, and then he surged out in a panic, leaves flying everywhere.

Elderberry had gone!

What had he been thinking the night before? How could he have told her that everyone at the holt thought she was dead? He had probably upset her too, saying harsh things about beavers, when she'd grown up thinking she was one. What did it matter if she didn't walk or stand like an otter? She was his sister. And he'd slept the most comfortable night he'd had since he left Greenriver in her strange little den. His mother – their mother – wasn't going to care if she was a strange sort of otter. She was just going to want Elderberry back. And he had chased her away on her own, probably straight into the jaws of the night wolf.

Sedge flung himself out on the riverbank, hissing with fright and fury. He had to find her. He couldn't believe that he had been so stupid. He stood among the reeds, nose quivering, desperately trying to catch Elderberry's scent. Had she gone downstream or up? He breathed deep, trying to calm himself, remembering the soft river scent of his sister's fur. Upstream? He thought so.

Sedge launched himself clumsily into the water and began to paddle as fast as he could. He had no idea how far ahead of him she was. But he was fast and fit after his journey downriver. He would catch her. He had to.

It was almost midday when Sedge came upon her hunting. He heard her before he saw her – the tell-tale splash of an otter diving under the surface. The river had scoured out a deep pool at a bend, and at first all he could see of her was bubbles, the air rising from her fur.

Sedge slipped quietly under the surface and watched her coiling and weaving through the waterweeds, turning on her tail as the fish jinked around her. She was so fast! He watched her admiringly, peering through the reed stems, and thought that he had never seen such a strong and graceful swimmer. There was a sharp swirl in the water as she seized a fat trout, and then she surfaced in triumph, popping up on to a rock near the bank to eat. Sedge followed her, putting his head out of the water cautiously. He suspected she wasn't going to be glad to see him.

'Oh. It's you.' His sister peered down at him. 'You followed me.' Then she glanced at the fish in between her front paws and hunched over, her ears flattening.

'I don't want any of it!' Sedge called quickly. 'I can catch my own. Just don't disappear again, please? Wait for me.' He dived neatly under the surface.

Silken went back to tearing into her trout and licking up the delicious orange eggs it had been about to lay, while keeping a curious eye on the other otter. She could see him as a shadow darting through the water, a trail of silver bubbles here and there. He seemed to swim quite like she did – a little more slowly, perhaps, but at least she hadn't been doing it completely wrong. And he ate fish! She had panicked, when he'd caught her biting into the trout. It was delicious, and she'd been so hungry, but Speckle and the others would have been disgusted. Otters did eat fish though, clearly. So that was all right.

He came surging out into the shallows to pin a wriggling trout on the pebbles next to her. His fish wasn't quite as large as hers, Silken noted, secretly proud.

'See?' he gasped. 'Not nicking yours.'

'Mmm.'

He took a few bites and sighed. 'I needed that. I've been chasing you upriver all morning.' He added quietly, 'I'm sorry. I didn't know what to say to you last night. You weren't what I expected.'

Silken tried to swallow a mouthful of fish but it seemed to stick in her throat. 'What did you expect?'

'I suppose I'd built it all up in my head that I was going on a quest, like I told you. I thought it would be different when I found you.' He scrabbled his claws in the pebbles, and looked up at her, shamefaced. 'I thought I'd know you straight away. And you'd know me. Maybe Lady River would appear and tell me that I'd done a great service. The two of us together would be able to see her. She might listen to us.' He gave her a quick, embarrassed look. 'Don't laugh at me!'

'I'm not. But I don't understand. Who's Lady River? Is that the same as the lady of the holt?'

Sedge was silent with shock. Didn't beavers know about Lady River? 'No,' he said at last. 'She *is* the river. Beavers don't have river ceremonies?'

Silken folded her paws. 'No. We – they – have dams. To shape the river. Not ceremonies.'

She sounded confused, and a little dismissive, Sedge thought. He swallowed hard.

'I didn't realise that,' he murmured. 'But – but I suppose I can explain it all to you before the full moon. There's time. Not a *lot* of time though. If we set off now, we should just about make it back for the ceremony, but it's a lot harder, swimming upstream. Especially at the moment. The river's risen so much, even in the time I've been travelling.'

'I'm not taking part in any ceremonies,' Silken said in a flat voice. 'I told you, I'm not Elderberry, though maybe I was *once*. I'm not even sure about that.'

'How can you think that? Haven't you listened to anything I've said?' Sedge pounded his paw on the shingle. 'We had the same dream!'

'That doesn't prove anything.'

Sedge growled furiously, stamping round in a circle. 'It does! You remember being flooded out!'

Silken shrugged. 'Perhaps. Or maybe we just both ate bad fish, and it gave us strange dreams. This ceremony doesn't mean anything to me. Why should I come back with you?'

'Because – because you have to,' Sedge begged. 'It's your *duty*. Can't you see how much the river's rising? We have to protect the holt.'

'It's not *my* holt, not *my* duty. Nothing to do with me. How can it be, when I don't even remember the place?' She'd had quite enough of expectations at Stronghold. Silken didn't plan on going and being a disappointment somewhere else.

'It remembers you,' Sedge told her quietly. 'Everyone does. Our mother most of all. They miss you. Look.' He stood up, putting a paw to the close fur around his neck, and pulled out a woven string, with something small and pale gleaming at the end. Then he yanked it over his head and passed it to her.

Silken peered at the pendant, not quite sure what she was supposed to be looking at. 'What is it, a river pearl?' It was larger than the tiny pearls she had seen used to decorate stitchwork at the lodge, but she couldn't think what else it could be. It was obviously precious, for him to wear it around his neck.

'It's one of your baby teeth. Our mother has one that she wears all the time too. So we can never forget that we lost you.' He sighed. 'Not that it worked. I did forget – I think I wanted to. Or maybe I was too frightened to remember. I don't know.'

Silken turned the pendant over and over in her paws. Her own tooth? It seemed very small.

The necklace twisted something inside her. She kept

wanting to chuckle to herself. Or was it that she wanted to whimper and whine? She couldn't tell. Her brother – her brother! – was watching her hopefully, his head on one side.

'I suppose you think now I'm going to come with you,' she hissed.

'Please!'

Silken saw him eyeing the necklace, and handed it back.

'You don't have to stay at the holt, if you don't like it,' he added, as he pulled it over his head again. 'Just come back and see where you were born. Let our mother and everyone know that you're safe, and then you can decide what you want to do. If I have to be lord of the holt after all, then I will,' he added glumly.

Silken eyed him suspiciously. 'What does that mean?'

'I'm our mother's heir, but only because you, um, aren't there. You're older than me. It should be you.'

Silken snorted. As if that was going to happen. 'That seems a very odd way of doing things. Why should you or I lead the holt just because our mother did?'

Sedge gazed back at her. 'Because that's what happens. That's how things *work*. One of us has to inherit. Our family are the leaders of the holt, it's been that way for ever.' He sighed. 'I didn't mean for it to be like this.'

'What did you want then?' Silken said.

He closed his eyes. 'I suppose I just assumed you'd be happy that I'd found you, and everyone at the holt would be happy with *me*.' Then he added, in a whisper, 'For once.'

Silken nodded knowingly. 'So it's all about you.'

Sedge didn't answer her. Instead he dived back into the deep river pool, and started to swim in wild circles and spirals, every so often shooting up out of the water and flinging himself back with a splash. Silken watched him and went back to eating her trout. She considered eating his too, but decided he'd probably want it when he'd finished working off his temper.

Eventually he stomped back out on to the shingle and started tearing at the fish in great huge bites.

'Feeling better?' Silken asked, licking her whiskers.

'No,' he growled back.

'I will come with you,' she told him, kicking the fishbones back into the water. 'Just to see. But don't get your hopes up.'

'All right,' he said, through a mouthful of fish. He looked relieved. 'At least then our mother will know that you're alive. And that Lady River has given you back. It's always felt to her as though the river stole you away, you see. Once she knows you're safe then perhaps she can talk to the river again. Perhaps she'll be able to sing back the flood.' He cast an anxious glance at the river tearing past, earth-darkened and swirling.

'She sings too? Our mother?' Silken asked him.

'Yes. She loved your songs, when you were tiny. She said that you'd be better than her when you'd grown, she was sure of it. She loved to sing too, but she only sings for the ceremonies now, only when she has to. Neither of us wanted to sing much, after we lost you.' Sedge glanced sideways, worried that he might have upset her again. But she seemed not to mind.

'Do all otters sing?'

'Most otters sing, but you made songs up,' Sedge tried to explain. 'That was different.' He saw her flinch, and stood up quickly, resting one front paw on the rock, and reaching the other up to her. 'I meant your songs were special, not that they were wrong!'

Silken turned her shoulder, and muttered, 'I got called different a lot back at Stronghold. It wasn't something anyone wanted to be, there.'

Sedge considered this, frowning. He complained about Greenriver all the time, although mostly just to himself. He hated feeling that he could never be as strong a leader as his mother. But he knew, from his lessons with Teasel, that the past lords and ladies of the holt had led their otters in very different ways. He had made up some of those rules and expectations for his own self. There wasn't a strict and perfect way to be an otter. Everyone worked for the good of the holt, but apart from that, otters lived as they pleased.

'I *think* all otters are different,' Sedge said hesitantly. 'I'm not much like Ma, but she doesn't mind, mostly.'

Silken settled back down on the rock, letting her own paw rest close to his. 'Our mother must be beside herself, with you gone.'

'I was doing it for her,' Sedge protested, but he knew it sounded thin. 'And they can't be angry with me for running off if I bring you back, can they?'

She snorted. Then she turned to look back downstream. 'No one knows where we are. We're free.'

Sedge followed her gaze. 'When I set out to find you, it felt wonderful, being away from the holt, and all my duties. At first, anyway. Do beavers know about the night wolf?'

Silken nodded. 'We – they, I mean – call her the old wolf, but I suppose it's the same story.'

'It's not a story,' Sedge muttered.

'You *saw* her?'

'Walked right past me.' Sedge couldn't help just the slightest hint of a boast in his voice. But then it faded away. 'I was so scared I didn't even breathe. I wanted my mother, Teasel, anyone. I wanted my holt.'

Silken remembered how frightened she had been when she'd heard the alarm call and thought it meant a wolf attack. She had wanted home too – and then home had been stolen away from her.

'I suppose you can't be an adventurer without a home waiting for you,' she said slowly. 'Without it you're just – lost.'

'You have a home,' Sedge promised her, and this time he scrambled right up on to the rock and settled next to her, gently nudging the very ends of her whiskers with his own.

They sat watching the water for a few moments. Then Sedge looked upstream. 'Shall we go? We don't have long.'

For answer, Silken slid into the water, and set off at a steady paddle. Sedge joined her, and they swam upriver together, a wake arrowing out behind them.

'Tell me about this ceremony then,' Silken said, once they'd rounded the bend of the river.

'It takes place at the full moon's rising. That's why we need to be back. We always hold the most important ceremonies at the full moon. Lots of the old stories tell that Lady River's a white otter, you see. It's the silver of the moonlight on the water that makes her, so they say. Our mother needs to beg for Lady River not to flood us out again.'

'Your home was flooded?'

'The holt is built under an ancient willow tree,' he said, realising that she didn't know. 'It's all tunnels and caves. The upper chambers are safe – they're hollowed back into the higher ground behind the tree. But the river's rising too quickly. The lower chambers are at risk.'

Silken nodded thoughtfully. 'My father – I mean – the beavers – they were worried about the dam. We were shoring it up. The water was coming downstream very fast, it all adds to the wear and tear.'

'Do the dams really stop the river?' Sedge asked curiously. 'Teasel – she's my tutor, yours too when you were little – she said beavers built dams, and underwater caverns and all sorts of clever things.'

'Oh, yes, that's all true,' Silken agreed. 'The water backs up behind the dam and that deepens the river to make a pool. The entrance to the lodge is there, underwater. It's protected, you see? No one can get in without the lodge knowing. My father . . . well, Master Grey, I mean. He was the best builder in the lodge. So he was picked to be the Master Builder. The others chose him.' Silken tried to keep the pride out of her voice – after all, Master Grey was *not* her father, not really – but she couldn't help a little of it seeping in.

'Perhaps we need something clever like that at the holt,' Sedge said thoughtfully. 'I don't know if it could survive being flooded out again. We're still scouring out some of the lower rooms from last time. If the flood weakens the bank, one of these days the willow tree might fall.'

Sedge glanced sideways at the banks of the river, the dull silver gleam of high water seeping through the grass, and he remembered the pale and reaching roots of the fallen willow, where he'd seen the night wolf. How high would the water be now, back at the holt? At least the heavy rains had subsided for the moment, even if there wasn't much sun. Hopefully the holt was safe for now. He didn't think they could swim any faster.

CHAPTER TWELVE

Along the river

Despite the urgency, and their fear of the night wolf, the journey back up the river was a joy to the two young otters. The weather had settled again, even though the river was still higher than it should be. They swam through sun-warmed water, deep and green and silky. The fishing was good, although Sedge missed the clever herbs and the ramsons that Bramble used back at the holt to season their meals.

'Your fur's growing sleeker,' he told his sister one morning, as they pulled their catch out on to the rocks at the edge of the river.

Silken looked down at herself in surprise. 'Is it?' She took a mouthful of fish and then glowered at him. 'What was wrong with my coat before?'

Sedge flinched, and crouched down silently over his meal, until she snorted in amusement.

'I was teasing you.'

'Oh. You look healthy, that was all I meant. Your fur looks glossy, and I can't see your bones like I could before.' He didn't add that she'd stopped hunching her shoulders to look like a beaver.

'I'm eating more fish, I suppose,' Silken said. 'I always wanted to but I had to hide it, back at the Stronghold. Beavers live on plants and tree bark. Grasses and leaves.'

She scratched at a bit of weed growing on the rock with her claw. 'I should have realised that I wasn't a beaver earlier.'

'You'd better eat the rest of this.' Sedge pushed his half-eaten fish towards her. 'I'm nearly full anyway. No fish! No wonder your fur looked patchy.'

'Patchy?' Silken growled. Then she darted out a paw and scooped the remains of her own fish into his face.

'Hey!' Sedge shook fishbones out of his whiskers. 'I was being nice!'

'I can catch my own, thank you! Patchy . . .' She showed her teeth at him. 'I'm a better fisher than you anyway.'

Silken lunged forward, nipping at his paws, and Sedge struck back, barging into Silken and knocking her into the river.

Silken surged up out of the water and launched herself at his throat, rolling him over in the shallows. The two otters wriggled and splashed, snapping at each other's necks. They slid in and out of holds and shot round the rocks to leap out at each other and wrestle all over again. At last they slumped down on the warm pebbles, their sides heaving.

'What happened to the rest of that fish?' Sedge asked, patting vaguely around the pebbles as though he might find it.

'Don't know. You kicked it in the river, I expect.'

'Huh.' Sedge closed his eyes, and let the sun warm his fur for a moment. Then he rolled over to look at her. 'Do beavers play-fight like that?'

'Mmm,' Silken said, sleepily remembering. 'But I never joined in that much. The beaver kits my age were heavier than I was. Frost would have squashed me if we wrestled.'

Sedge snorted. 'Yeah, like Pebble and me.'

'Frost was my friend though. He stuck up for me. Speckle did too.'

'Do you miss them?' Sedge asked her.

'Yes. But I couldn't stay. I didn't belong, even before I knew I was an otter.'

'Maybe one day you could go downstream again,' Sedge suggested doubtfully. He wanted to keep her safely at the holt for ever, but perhaps he was being selfish, and she sounded so wistful. 'You could go and see them for a visit.' Then he thought of Teasel telling him about beavers and their strange ways, and wondered if beavers said the same sort of thing about otters. Would Silken be welcome again in a beaver lodge, once they knew what she was?

It had been glorious, escaping from the close, suffocating love and expectation at the holt, but he couldn't imagine never being allowed to go back home. Realising that home had never been a home would be even worse.

Hesitantly, he edged closer to Silken and pressed his back against hers. They were both curled up, so only a tiny scrap of his fur touched hers. If she didn't want him there, she could twitch apart in a moment. But Silken didn't move away. Instead the rigid curve of her spine sagged, and she pressed a little closer. Neither of them said anything more. Each cub lay listening to the other breathing, and after a while they slept.

A few days into the journey, the heavy spring rains came back, and they were somehow even harder to bear after the respite. There seemed to be nowhere warm and dry to shelter, and Sedge and Silken were cold to the bone. Swimming felt harder with thick, cold paws and heavy fur, and the river was in full spate.

Several times they had to twist suddenly to avoid branches and other debris tumbling through the water, and the constant vigilance was exhausting. They were slower now too. Each night Sedge watched the moon creeping back towards fullness and worried. What would happen if they missed the ceremony? Could it be put off until the next full moon? Was there time?

'What is it?' Silken asked, watching him peer out from under the bramble thicket where they were sheltering. The rain clouds were slashing across the sky and the fleeting glimpses of the moon showed that it was almost round.

Sedge turned back to look at her. 'Thought I heard something, that's all. Ever since I saw the wolf, I keep thinking I can hear her coming. It's stupid.' He sighed. 'And we're taking too long. Two more nights until the moon is full? Three?'

'Three maybe,' Silken agreed, wriggling forward to look. 'It's hard to tell with all that rain.'

Sedge groaned, circling round the little nest they'd mounded up in the fallen leaves under the bramble vines. 'The river's going to be faster tomorrow, and higher. Harder to swim. It's slowing us up.'

Silken watched him stomp through the leaf litter for a moment more, and then she stuck out her paw, so that he almost tripped over her. 'Stop it,' she said. 'You're tearing yourself apart. The old wolf's far away by now, and we're going as fast as we can. We need to rest, and groom. We can sleep now and set out again later tonight if it's stopped raining.' She shoved him firmly down into the leaves, and then started to groom him, clawing the dirt and damp out of his fur. Sedge was so surprised that he lay still under her paws, listening to her mutter and growl.

'I should do the same for you,' he murmured at last, but she only shushed him. Her paws were moving more slowly now, smoothing down his fur, and she began to sing in time.

> *Pale dry sedge grass,*
> *In the wind it sings,*
> *Pale dry sedge grass,*
> *Whispers secret things.*

The words twisted in and out of the pattering of raindrops, hissing and murmuring. Sedge sighed, some of the fear easing out of his bones.

Then he coiled under her paws, whipping round to face her. 'You remembered it!'

'Sit still!'

Obediently he turned away again, but he peered round at her over his shoulder. 'You never said.'

'It only came back to me today. I had the elderberry verse in my head all that time, and then suddenly there was this one there too.' Her paws stilled on his fur for a moment. Perhaps I'm starting to remember,' she said. 'Tiny flashes of memories keep coming back to me, but they don't always stay.'

'What sort of things?' Sedge asked eagerly.

'A crown of flowers.' Silken's muzzle wrinkled. 'It kept falling down over my eyes . . .'

'That would be from one of the ceremonies,' Sedge said. 'We took part in them even when we were small. We used to carry baskets of petals to throw on the water.'

'And there was singing? All the memories seem to have singing.'

'Always,' Sedge agreed.

'Singing . . . seems important,' Silken murmured. 'Elderberry knew that it was. Even when she was tiny.'

Sedge waited silently for her to go on, even though it was odd to hear her talk of Elderberry as someone else. He wondered if she would ever be able to join Elderberry and Silken back together.

'Perhaps when we get back to the holt, I could help your mother sing to the river,' she murmured, stroking her claws through his fur again. 'I could make a new song, about the water.' Then she added suddenly, 'The crown kept falling down my nose, but I loved it. I remember that.'

'The ceremonies go on for ever, and the crowns look stupid,' Sedge said. 'But sometimes there's a moment when it all seems right. When it almost feels as if Lady River's there with us listening. It's the songs – she listens to the songs if we mean them, I know she does. She'll listen to you, Silken.'

The two otters lay there under the brambles, looking out at the water churning past, pitted by raindrops. Silken began to sing again, a song that rolled and bounced along like the dashing water.

> *Dashing and tumbling*
> *Rolling and rumbling*
> *The river goes on!*
>
> *Seething and pattering*
> *Nattering chattering*
> *The rain goes on!*

She'd begun quietly, stopping and starting as she fumbled for the words, but then Sedge joined in, growling a stormy bass line as he drummed his paws, and her words came more swiftly, and stronger. Her song was carried away on the wind and the rain, and slowly, Sedge noticed other listeners gathering round – and even in – their bramble thicket.

There was a tiny bird, feathers fluffed out against the wet, perched on a thorny branch above Silken's nose. He was watching her, moonlight sparkling in his dark jewel eyes. Every so often Sedge caught a thin bright chirp, but most of the bird's song was blown away by the storm. A squirrel was watching from the tree branches hanging out over the water. There were whispers and hisses, and the padding of small paws close by.

Then, from downstream, Sedge caught a faint whistling sound. He thought for a moment that it was the wind changing direction and echoing in the trees, until he caught a pale shape arrowing towards them over the water.

'What is that?' he whispered. Next to him Silken's voice died away and she wriggled out of the brambles to look too.

'I think . . .' she whispered, trailing off as the white shape slid down to the water, kicking up a mass of spray as it skated over the surface. Sedge stepped back, thinking that the great bird was about to blunder straight into them, but its wild landing smoothed out into a steady glide across the water.

'Is that a swan?' Sedge gasped. Even though the bird was paddling smoothly across the river now, he still didn't want to get near it. Swans were fierce.

Silken was slipping into the water, ignoring him.

'Come back!' Sedge hissed. 'Silken, he's dangerous, don't go near him!' He slid into the river after her, thinking that perhaps two of them together might frighten the great creature off. Then he stopped, staring at his sister as she coiled and splashed around the swan, nudging affectionately at his crisp feathers.

'You seem happier than when we last met,' the swan said, or Sedge thought he did. The swan's voice was harsh and creaking, and he had to fight to understand the words.

'I found an otter,' Silken told the swan, nodding at Sedge. 'He thinks – well, he says he's my brother.'

Sedge sniffed. Silken could sound a little more enthusiastic about it, he thought. She beckoned him closer.

'The swan is a friend,' she explained. 'His nest isn't far from the beaver lodge, and he knows the river, and everything that happens on it. I went to him after I saw the raft otters. I thought he would be able to tell me how I'd ended up at Stronghold as a kit.'

'Cub,' Sedge muttered, but he nodded politely at the swan.

'He told me about the Greenriver otters,' Silken explained. 'He was the one who sent me travelling upriver.'

'I think I've heard of you!' Sedge said excitedly, paddling a little nearer. 'I talked to a kingfisher on my journey down the river. He told me that there was a great swan who lived in a grove of birches, and he would know where to find my sister, if anyone did.'

'Did he now,' said the swan. He snaked his neck down to examine Sedge, who tried very hard not to flinch, and almost managed it. 'Are you still making for the holt?' he asked, turning back to Silken.

'Yes,' Silken said. She looked worried. 'You said that I should.'

'I still think you should, small one, but you must go faster. Look at the river. It was like this last spring.' A shiver ran through him, ruffling up his feathers. 'You must get yourselves safely under cover at the holt as soon as you can. I've heard rumours that the wolf is travelling along the river again, driven out of her den by the rising water. You're too small to be out alone, the pair of you.'

'Sedge saw the wolf,' Silken whispered, and the old swan drew back his neck, his wing-feathers rustling.

'It was days ago. She must be far away by now,' Sedge said uneasily.

'We've only stopped for a short while to rest,' Silken added. 'We'll set out again soon.'

'Good, good,' the swan hissed. Then he went on, 'I'm glad I found you again. I heard your singing carried on the wind. You sing well together. I couldn't help but follow the sound.

I suppose you might – would you – hmmm.' He let out an odd whooping noise that made the otters start back in surprise – and then Silken realised that he was embarrassed. 'My mate and I used to sing together. Would you sing again? For me?'

Silken stared at him, and then glanced sideways at Sedge in shy delight. Sedge nodded.

'What shall we sing?' she asked, and the swan nibbled and clacked at his wing-feathers for a moment.

'Anything.'

The otters scrambled out on to the damp mud in front of the bramble thicket, and the old swan hopped after them. He settled himself at the very edge of the bank, curling into a ball of feathers and tucking his beak under his wing to listen.

Silken began with the song they had been singing before, the bright tune settling to the rhythm of the raindrops on the water, but soon the song changed to something softer and darker. She could feel Sedge and the old swan and the other silent listeners around her, all frightened, all cold, all rain-soaked, and she sang for them.

> *River, won't you feed us,*
> *Each and every day,*
> *River, won't you help us,*
> *Safe by your waters stay.*

Sedge was right beside her, trembling as he hummed along. Silken was singing to the river now, she realised, in a way she never had before. Sedge's certainty had persuaded her that Lady River might listen – that there was someone there in the water *to* listen.

Her voice faltered. Was this allowed, here in the darkness and the rain? Two small otters, and a grumpy swan, and who knew how many creatures gathered behind them in the brambles and bracken? Didn't she need garlands, and a court of otters? She glanced at Sedge, and saw that his eyes were wide, but he waved a paw at her and whispered, 'Go on!'

Silken hesitated a moment, letting the dark dread from her nightmares fill her words.

> *River, still we need you,*
> *Each and every day,*
> *River, now we fear you,*
> *Don't sweep our homes away.*

Silken could feel a shivering silence all around her, beyond her circle of listeners. She had always sung for herself before. Now she felt so many others swept up in her words.

Sedge crept even closer, pressing up against her side as she went on.

River, please protect us,
Each and every day,
River, wrap around us,
Care for every stray.

She could hear Sedge's teeth chattering together, and he'd stopped singing, but his warmth against her side was comforting. She was trying to find the perfect words – she almost had it. There was something listening to their song, Silken could tell. The rain had stopped battering on the water, and the wind had died down. The silence was listening.

'*River, please protect us,*' she whispered, her voice shaking, and she heard Sedge echo her words, and then the old swan too, and a chorus of tiny whispers after.

'*River, please protect us . . .*'

The silence lasted a moment longer, and then the wind began to hiss and howl again. But the water stayed strangely calm.

'Go now,' the old swan said, watching the river. 'Get back home now, small ones. Take all our wishes with you. Speak for us.'

'We'll try,' Silken told him, and then she turned to Sedge. 'Can you go on?'

Sedge slipped into the water. 'We must.'

Silken dived after him and felt the water wrap around her, soft and cool. She turned back to look at the swan, still on the bank. 'Will we ever see you again? I don't even know your name.'

He rose to his feet. 'Perhaps I will travel upriver one day. My name is Vane. My mate was Quill. I would be grateful if you would remember her, when you tell the story of that day.'

'Always,' Silken murmured. 'How could I forget?'

CHAPTER THIRTEEN

On the river,

just downstream from the Holt

The strength from the song lasted one long night's swim, and half into the next day. And by that evening, Sedge was back in the stretch of the river that he knew.

'We should make the holt tomorrow,' he said, as he and Silken panted for breath on the bank. They were huddled under a stand of bracken as the rain rattled and hammered around them, watching the river race by. They had dragged themselves out of the water a few moments before, exhausted. It was earlier than they had wanted to stop, but they were too worn out to keep on swimming when the river was so fast.

'I've never seen it like this,' Sedge muttered. 'I've swum this part of the river before when I was collecting water plants for the healers, but it all looks different now. The banks have changed.' He twisted his paws together, chittering anxiously.

What if he was taking Silken back to a holt that was already gone? Sedge shook himself. They had to carry on, whatever had happened. They had given their word. Something of the holt would still be there, surely. One last sleep, and then one last swim. They could be at the holt by morning.

'We need to find somewhere dry to sleep,' Silken said. 'I'm so cold that I can't remember ever not being cold.'

He nudged his sister. 'What about that tree up there? It's hollow, I think. There might be enough room to sleep inside.'

'All right,' Silken said. 'I suppose it's got to be drier than out here.'

The trunk had split in two long ago, and there was a dusty hole just above the roots.

'Seems dry enough,' Sedge said, nosing about. 'The wind's blowing the rain the other way. It'll do for the night.'

They squeezed themselves inside, listening to the river thundering past, a tail's length away. Silken lay with her muzzle at the opening of the hole, sure that she would never sleep. She kept on thinking it as Sedge pillowed his head on her side, and then as her eyes closed and she dream-scrabbled at the dusty bark. The two exhausted young otters slept as the rain slashed down, and the river began to rise again around them.

Sedge and Silken dreamed time back together. Last spring's golden evening sunlight faded as the clouds drew in. The water started to swirl and hurry through the tunnels of the holt as the tiny cubs squirmed and dreamed. The flood tore into their sleeping chamber and swept them out into the dark river, spluttering and terrified.

Sedge muttered and wriggled and fought to wake up. He reached again for Elderberry – or was it Silken? – and felt panic as their paws touched and pulled away. The water was filling his mouth, his nose, his eyes, and then he splashed back above the surface and screamed.

'Elderberry! Silken! It's not a dream, wake up!' He paddled frantically with paws that felt like bent sticks, fighting against the water to reach his sister. He could see her, so close by, her eyes silvery in the moonlight. She was swimming in the same weak, dazed way that he was, trying to get some sort of grip on the water. The two young otters stretched towards each other, and Sedge kicked wildly, determined that this time he would not let her go. He ploughed towards Silken, thrashing and sputtering. He almost had hold of her when he saw her eyes change, widening to great circles of fear.

And then all he saw was darkness as a great branch came tumbling out of nowhere and struck him across the head.

Silken screeched in terror as Sedge rolled sickeningly backwards and disappeared under the branch. She dived just in time to save herself, and the swirling river caught and spun her, driving her out of the flood and crushing her against the tree they had been sleeping in.

Silken clung tightly to the bark, digging in her claws as the water seethed around her. The wild wave drained away, leaving her perched in the crook of two branches. Silken lay there for a moment, her sides heaving as she coughed up river and slime. Then she called frantically for her brother, searching across the water for his neat round head.

'Sedge! Sedge! Where are you? Sedge, answer me!'

No answer came. There was no sign of him.

Except – was that debris swirling in a strange eddy halfway across the river, or could it be a small otter body? With a grim hiss of fright, Silken leaped down from the branches and paddled furiously between the flooded trees until she was well upstream of the clump of debris. Then she flung herself back into the raging central channel of the river, and let the flood carry her on a wild ride back down to find him. She had never tried to swim in water so fast. It whirled her along, flinging her this way and that.

There! At last she saw her brother by a stand of pale birches, turning slowly over and over in the swirling water, limp as a torn leaf. Something cold settled inside her. Not now.

Not when they'd only just found each other. When she was only just starting to remember . . .

Silken struck out, swimming with the last of her strength for the knot of timber and reeds and rubbish spinning in a dark whirlpool in the middle of the river.

She plunged into the heart of the mass and grabbed Sedge by the scruff of his neck. The strange current tried to hold on to him, and to capture Silken too, but she was too angry and savage to be caught.

'Give him back! Give him back to me *now*!' she snarled. Did she imagine a moment of still surprise? There was definitely a faint slackening in the pull of the water. She dived at once, dragging Sedge down through the depths and out of the maelstrom to calmer water below.

Surfacing, Silken ploughed grimly to the riverbank – which wasn't at all where it was meant to be – swimming through the shallow floodwater, trailing Sedge beside her until she reached half-solid ground. Sedge sagged horribly into the mud as she laid him down, his head lolling to one side, eyes half open.

'Wake up!' Silken hissed, patting at his muzzle, gently at first, and then harder and harder as she became more desperate. 'Sedge, wake up! Breathe! Please!'

'He's gone,' someone said behind her. A massive dark

head came down beside her own and a white-flecked snout nudged her brother's limp paws.

The voice spoke again. 'Dead.' Then it added, 'Lucky for him.'

Silken turned, looking up at the wolf towering above her.

Fear flooded her body. She tried to skid sideways, out of reach of those great jaws, but the wolf only hissed appreciatively and brought one massive paw down on the end of Silken's tail, pinning her to the wet ground. Silken thrashed and twisted, but she couldn't get away. She snarled, trying to sound defiant, but the wolf merely lowered her head, fixing her with one blazing golden eye. The other was cast over with a whitish film, and Silken guessed that it was blind. One eye was enough – the gold fire seemed to have Silken frozen. She lay in the mud, panting and terrified, gazing back at the wolf.

'Were you following us?' she whispered. 'Sedge thought he heard you – I said he was imagining things.'

The wolf snorted, and planted the other paw on Silken's shoulder, crushing her into the ground.

The little otter yowled, trying to squirm away, but the wolf only pressed harder. She lowered her head, and Silken saw a thread of drool gather around her sagging gums. The wolf's teeth were loose. The beavers were right, she *was*

old – ancient and half blind and starving. Probably she was relying on carrion and stupid prey. Like two young otters who weren't paying enough attention because they were desperate to make it home.

Blackness was seeping in at the edges of Silken's eyes now. She tried one last time to fight, to wriggle out from under the massive paws, but she couldn't move. She was being squashed into a muddy death, but it didn't hurt any more.

Then all at once the weight on her chest seemed to disappear, and Silken sucked in a huge breath. Pain came rushing back as something crashed heavily into the mud beside her.

Silken blinked away the dark mist and looked up at her brother, who was standing over her clutching a rock. Very, very slowly, she rolled her head sideways. There was the body of the wolf, so close beside her that Silken could see the golden fire, still dying in that one eye. She looked away again, quickly.

'How did you . . .?' she rasped.

Sedge looked at the rock in his paws and then dropped it into the mud next to the wolf. 'She was crouching down to bite you, otherwise I'd never have been able to reach. I think she's dead. I thought *you* were dead.'

'So did I,' Silken muttered, shaking out each paw in turn to see if they all still worked. 'You saved me.'

'You pulled me out of the river. We're even, we saved each other.' Sedge eyed Silken worriedly. 'Did she break any bones? She was crushing you.' He stroked Silken's muzzle and her ears, trying to comfort her, but Silken just stared at him, her eyes wide and wondering.

'What is it?' Sedge demanded.

'I remember,' she said quietly. 'Perhaps it was being caught in the flood with you again. Or the wolf half throttling me. But I remember . . . you.'

'You know that you're my sister!' Sedge bounced on all four paws, darting round her. 'You know that you're Elderberry!'

'Yes,' Silken said dazedly. 'Yes, I suppose I am. But I still feel like Silken. Elderberry is – someone else.'

Sedge stopped jumping and came to nuzzle close against her. 'You don't have to be Elderberry,' he whispered. 'Silken belongs to the holt too.'

Sedge and Silken left the great body lying in the mud where it had fallen. It was too big for them to bury, and besides, the other creatures of the river would want to know that the wolf was gone. By the time Silken had caught her breath and let

Sedge clean the worst of the mud out of her coat, the birds in the trees above them were already calling the news excitedly up and down the banks.

The two otters half waded, half swam through the floodwaters, weaving their way around trees and clotted heaps of debris that had washed down the river.

'Do you remember any more?' Sedge asked after a while.

'I – I think so. But it feels so strange. As if I had two lives, and now they're being squashed back on top of each other. I couldn't remember being very small at the beaver lodge, but I thought that I *must* have been – that I didn't remember only because I was little. I imagined myself there. When the others spoke about being kits, I saw myself doing the things they remembered. Now I know that none of that was real. But I can't get rid of those pictures in my head.'

Silken frowned to herself as they squelched onwards. She remembered it all now.

She remembered huddling dazedly behind the swan's crisp white feathers, listening as he stood outside the lodge at the Stronghold, calling loudly for the Master Builder. When a furry head had popped up irritably out of the pool at last, she had flinched back at such strangeness.

'What is it? Can't you see we're busy? Repairs to make, everywhere's a mess.' Then the creature had shaken himself, sending water droplets shimmering from spikes of brown fur, and lumbered closer with a sigh. 'I'm sorry. So much damage. What is it, old friend?'

Silken had squeaked in fear as the old swan scooped his wing around her and pushed her forward.

'I had nowhere else to take her. Do what you will with her. I can't stay. My mate . . .' The swan gave an odd, desperate croak. 'I have to find her to bury. I have to keep searching. Look after the kit, Master Grey.'

Then he had beaten his great wings so powerfully that Silken was slammed against the beaver's side as the swan took off. She found herself nestling into damp fur, comforting and yet unfamiliar.

'And where did he find you, small one?' the creature had murmured, peering down at her. 'Where do you belong?'

Numb with fear and weariness and want, Silken hadn't been able to speak. She'd merely shaken her head and then buried her nose in his fur again.

And he had taken her in.

'They were very kind,' she said to Sedge now. 'He named me Silken. I suppose beaver fur is different – thicker and longer. My pelt must have seemed very slight and soft to them.'

'At home, you were named Elderberry because your fur

was dark and reddish, like the berries,' Sedge told her, and Silken looked down at her dark paws shyly.

'What colour is our mother's fur?' she asked. 'A – a tawny brown?'

'Yes!' Sedge splashed a little in his excitement. 'The colour of may thorns, just a little darker than mine. Do you remember what our father looked like?'

'His coat was grey . . .'

Sedge nodded. 'The colour of smoke.'

'I suppose . . . if my fur is an unusual colour, it might help our mother to recognise me,' Silken said.

Sedge frowned. 'She'll know you, Silken. I'm sure of it. If I'd seen you in the daylight, I would have known at once that you were an otter. I still feel foolish that I didn't realise who you were straight away, especially when I was trying to find you.'

Silken shrugged. 'You thought I must be a beaver, so you saw a beaver. I thought the same.' She looked ahead through the trees. 'How much further do you think it is?'

'We should be there today.' Sedge swerved round a pile of fallen branches.

'And the ceremony?' Silken asked. 'Will we be in time?'

'I'm almost sure tonight's the full moon. We'll make it.'

Sedge knew that he had been right to go – he had found his lost sister. Nevertheless, a cold feeling settled inside. As they came closer to the holt, he kept thinking how frightened his mother must be to have *both* her children gone.

I'm coming, he wanted to scream to her. *I am, I promise. I'm almost home. You'll be glad I went.*

As the afternoon began to turn to evening, Sedge and Silken came silently around the last bend in the river before the holt. The light was low and golden bright on the water, the sky a soft grey like the inside of a mussel shell.

The holt was empty. There were no old otters perched gossiping in the tree roots, no little ones jumping and splashing in the shallows at the bankside. The old willow tree was marooned in a rippling sheet of golden floodwater.

'Where are they?' Sedge shot forward, sick inside. He scanned the banks for Lily, for Tormentil, for his mother. Had they left, been driven out by the flood? Or . . . had they not left in time?

Sedge dipped under the water, paddling through the grey dimness, dreading that he'd see the broken shapes of otters. But the river was full only of silt and sticks. He surfaced, his heart seeming to swing wildly inside his chest. Perhaps if they searched further upstream . . .

'Where is everyone?' Silken asked.

'I don't know!' Sedge could hear the panic in his voice. He had brought her back, for this . . .

'Sedge!' A figure barrelled round the massive willow trunk, splashing through the floodwater, and then Teasel was flinging herself into the deeper part of the river. She had dived so badly that there wasn't so much a ripple as a wave, half swamping Sedge and Silken, so that they were spluttering even before Teasel seized Sedge in her jaws and began to shake him to and fro.

'Stop – it – stop – it – ow –' Sedge spat.

'Get off him!' Silken attempted to pull Teasel away, but the big old otter swatted at her as if she were a fly. Then she stopped abruptly, still gripping Sedge by the scruff of his neck, and stared at her.

'Who are you?' she demanded, round a mouthful of fur. And then, turning back to Sedge, 'Where have you been, you little scrub? Your mother's beside herself.'

'Look at her!' Sedge panted. 'Teasel, look at her!'

'Where did you find another cub?' Teasel growled. 'I suppose she's one of the raft otters. So now we'll have them descending on us, wanting to know why our stupid little lordling's absconded with one of their pups!'

'Let go of my brother,' Silken said coldly and, incredibly, Teasel did as she said. She dropped Sedge, who half sank under the surface before bobbing up again like a duckling. Teasel looked at Silken properly for the first time, her eyes bulging. She lifted one slow paw and reached out, as if touching Silken would help her believe that she was really there. But she couldn't quite bring herself to stroke this strange pup's muzzle.

'Elderberry?' she murmured. Then she wheeled round to glare at Sedge. 'You went to find Elderberry?'

'Yes.' Sedge hung his head. 'I know I should have told someone . . .'

'Young and foolish,' Teasel said, but she didn't sound angry any more. She looked beyond the great willow tree and yelled so loudly and suddenly that Silken flinched. Sedge, who had more experience of Teasel, only closed his eyes. 'My Lady Thorn! Come and see what I've found!'

Sedge opened his eyes again so he could roll them at Silken. 'You'd think *she'd* found you all herself,' he muttered.

'You two follow me, and we'll have less of that, little lord pup. Not sure I'm done shaking you yet. Try and look bright and cheerful, for Lady River's sake, your mother thinks you're dead.' She added to Silken, 'And she *knows* you're dead.'

Teasel set off, plunging through the flooded woodland towards the higher, drier ground.

The sound of splashing echoed through the waterlogged trees, and then they rounded a patch of damp scrub, and

Sedge saw his mother standing there. Thorn looked haggard and stooped, and surely there hadn't been so much silver around her muzzle when he had left?

Teasel chivvied Sedge and Silken to the bank, but both cubs hung back, staring at their mother.

'Sedge?' Thorn whispered, coming closer.

'I brought her back, Ma.' He hadn't called his mother that since Elderberry had gone, but now it seemed right. 'I found Elderberry. Except now her name is Silken,' he added hastily.

'Elderberry? But . . . how?' Thorn held out her paws to her daughter and Sedge saw that they were shaking.

'She was at the beaver lodge. The Stronghold,' Sedge explained. 'They took her in and raised her there. She never knew she was an otter.'

Thorn looked back and forth between the cubs as though she couldn't believe that there were two of them.

'I saw the raft otters go by one day,' Silken said quietly, lifting her eyes to look at her mother. 'Until then I didn't understand what I was.'

For a moment all of them were still, and then Thorn surged forward, shoving through the bracken and weeds and into the water. Sedge could see her eyes shining with fear and love and hope as she swam towards them. He felt Silken press close against his side, and he was sure he could hear her heart thundering deep under her fur.

Their mother seized Silken and clung to her lovingly, nuzzling and sniffing and holding her so tight. 'It *is*,' she murmured. 'It is my Elderberry, all grown.'

She led Silken out on to a patch of drier ground, and then drew Sedge to her. 'You did this for us,' she whispered, pulling him close. 'How did you know where she was?'

Sedge squirmed. Her grip on him was so hard it was almost painful. This was what he had wanted; for his mother to praise him. To show that she loved him. So why was he so embarrassed? 'I kept dreaming about the flood,' he said. 'Ma, that's not important now. You have to hear Silken sing. She makes her own songs.'

'As a tiny cub you sang more often than you spoke. I loved to listen to you,' Thorn murmured, gazing hungrily at Silken.

Silken shook her head. 'I don't really know how otters sing. I could be doing everything wrong. Beavers don't sing, you see. It was one of the things that made me different.'

'Beavers,' Teasel muttered, wrinkling her muzzle. 'Still. They seem to have looked after you well enough.'

More otters were popping up all around them now, drawn by Teasel's shouting. There were whispers and jumping and clapping of paws.

'Sedge is back!'

'But who's that with him? Is it – is it Elderberry?'

'How can it be?'

'He found her!'

'She's come back to us!'

'I told you he'd be home by the full moon,' Teasel said smugly to Thorn.

'Did you?' Sedge looked at her in surprise. 'You thought that I'd be back?'

Teasel shook her head. 'No. I *knew* you'd be back.'

Something twisted inside Sedge. All that time he had thought that Teasel couldn't wait to be rid of him. He shook himself, looking back through the trees at the deserted holt, and the shining expanse of water spread around it. He laid a paw on his mother's fur. 'The flood's still rising, isn't it?'

'Yes. We're going to have to abandon the holt.' His mother glanced around at the otters curled together under the trees, most with tiny bundles of snatched belongings that were all they had been able to save. 'So many generations of otters have lived at Greenriver and now we must start again. This is a cruel homecoming for you both.' She sounded exhausted, and Sedge and Silken moved together to hold her as she swayed on her feet.

'Listen, Ma. Silken sang to Lady River. I'm sure the river heard. She calmed the water for us, so we could swim upriver, so we could get here in time.'

'Truly?' Thorn straightened up, gazing at them with a desperate wonder in her eyes.

'We sang to her together,' Silken said firmly. 'It was both of us – and there were others listening. The old swan who first found me after the flood . . .'

'Other birds too, and some mice. A squirrel. And a weasel, I think,' Sedge agreed. 'They were gathering in the bushes.'

'A weasel?' Teasel sounded disgusted.

'The river belongs all of us,' Sedge told her. 'Everyone there was cold and desperate and scared.'

Teasel wrinkled her muzzle, but she didn't argue.

'You're right.' Lady Thorn sounded tired still, but determined. 'We all live on one river, whatever creatures we are. I have wondered, in the past, whether it was wrong to speak to the river just for ourselves. It isn't only the holt we should be trying to save.' She looked at her two cubs. 'Tonight is the full moon. Will you show me how to sing to her again?'

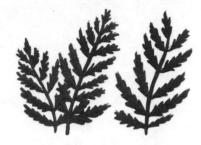

CHAPTER FOURTEEN

Greenriver, on the bank by the Holt

'I'm sorry that I brought you back to *this*,' Sedge said quietly to Silken. 'I promised you a holt, not another damp hole under a bramble bush.'

Their mother and Teasel had gone to pass on the news of the young otters' return to the scattered remnants of the holt, and to explain that the ceremony was to go ahead at moonrise. They'd left Sedge and Silken to rest, and ready themselves for the work of the night. Thorn had wrapped a blanket around each of them, drawing them close and nuzzling her soft whiskers in theirs.

His sister pulled the blanket up under her nose. 'It doesn't matter. Why didn't you tell them the old wolf is gone?'

Sedge was silent for a moment. 'I didn't know how,' he said at last. 'I hit her with a rock. That's not like fishing. It was different. I felt the life go out of her. She only wanted to eat. And she was old, Silken. She must have known so many things. We've lost all of that now.'

'She wasn't just a hunter,' Silken said gently. 'She killed more than she needed. That's what all the stories said, back at the lodge. The wolf was savage, and angry. And you only killed her to stop her hurting *me*.' Then she nudged him. 'Sedge, look.'

Two tiny otters were lurking next to a slim birch trunk, peering round it. 'Why are they staring?' Silken whispered. Was she going to be seen as an outsider wherever she went?

'You're exciting,' Sedge pointed out. 'You lived in a beaver lodge – and you travelled the river too. You're an adventurer. She won't bite you, you know,' he called to Willow and Marigold, who disappeared completely behind the tree with squeaks of shyness. Sedge patted his sister's paw. 'They'll get used to you. You'll wish they hadn't; they'll be climbing all over you, demanding songs about beavers and swans and daring rescues.'

'Daring rescues from enormous wolves,' Silken put in slyly. 'Maybe.'

Silken watched the little otters for another moment – or their muzzles and dark eyes, which was all that she could see around the birch tree – and then ducked her head. She curled herself with her back against their own sheltering tree, huddling the warm blanket up around her, and began to sing her song, her Elderberry song, darting her eyes sideways every so often to see how the little ones reacted.

Ripe black elderberries,
Gleaming in the sun.
Ripe black elderberries,
Enough for everyone.

Pale dry sedge grass,
In the wind it sings.
Pale dry sedge grass,
Whispers secret things.

By the time she'd reached the end of the second verse, the two tiny cubs were sitting in front of her, tugging at her blanket. Blinking in surprise, Silken let them snuggle in next to her, and went on singing. The cubs joined in, singing with her, their voices squeaky and small, until they fell asleep curled against her side.

'You see,' Sedge whispered, as Silken stopped with a quiet sigh after the seventh or eighth sing-through. 'I told you. I wouldn't let their mothers see that though. You'll be singing them to sleep every night.'

Silken felt a surprising happiness. After her bitter

encounters with Tawny and Brindle, there was a great melancholy sweetness to the soft weight of the babies curled up under her paws.

Sedge and Silken and the cubs dozed on the damp ground, and their dreams were quiet and strange. Silken walked upright along the riverbank, paw in paw with a shining white otter, and Sedge climbed alone in the elder tree, until his sister came to sit among the branches and sing.

'Wake up! Sedge! Come on, lazy.'

Sedge grabbed at the flailing branches of his dream tree – and then realised that he was already curled up on the ground and grunted himself awake.

Tormentil and Lily were pulling at his blanket. Silken was awake and looking nervously at his friends, and the two tiny cubs were still making little whistly snores up against her.

'Why didn't you tell us that you were going downriver?' Tormentil said, pretending to swipe at his ears.

'We'd have come with you!' Lily said.

Sedge nodded. 'I know you would. But I had to go on my own.'

Lily and Tormentil turned to stare at Silken. They both

bowed their heads, and Sedge saw Silken hunch her shoulders, that way she had when he'd first met her.

'Don't,' he murmured, nudging her. 'And don't you two do that either,' he added to Lily and Tormentil. 'You know her. You don't need to bow.'

'Do you remember us?' Lily asked curiously, and Silken nodded.

'I think so. More of my memories are coming back, now that I'm here. I remember Flint too, and – Pebble?'

'My brother.' Lily sighed. 'He's sulking back there somewhere. My parents set up camp by an old fallen tree. We left Flint there trying to coax him out of his temper. Everyone needs to be on their best behaviour for tonight.'

'I suppose he hoped I wasn't coming back,' Sedge muttered, and no one said anything for a moment.

Then Lily nodded. 'Maybe. But the rest of us are glad you're home. And that you are too,' she added shyly to Silken. 'I wish – I wish you'd had a better homecoming.'

'How bad is it?' Sedge asked. 'I couldn't ask my mother. She looked so – broken.'

Lily and Tormentil glanced at each other, and then Tormentil said slowly, 'Everyone got out. But the holt . . . The main chamber, the kitchen, the storerooms, they're all washed out. It's a mess.'

'I'm not even sure what this ceremony tonight can do. I don't know if we can stay,' Lily said.

The four young otters gazed at each other silently for a moment, and then Lily shook herself. 'Your mother sent us to bring you these.' She grinned at Sedge and turned to pick up an armful of greenery. 'I know how much you like a wreath.'

Sedge groaned as Lily and Tormentil held up wreaths of meadowsweet, white and frothy. It reminded him of the thick, bubbling foam that had clotted around the branches in the river the night before. Even without that he would have hated them. He could see at once that they would be itchy, and he would look ridiculous.

Tormentil set the wreath gently above his ears and giggled. 'Very fetching.'

'They're supposed to shine in the moonlight,' Lily explained. 'I think they'll look nice.' She held up the other wreath to Silken. 'Can I?' she asked, and Silken nodded.

The white flowers made Silken's fur seem even darker, Sedge noticed. She looked striking, rather than silly. The fluffy meadowsweet was drooping over his nose, and the tiny petals made him want to sneeze. But Willow and Marigold had woken now, and they were blinking up at Sedge and Silken in their wreaths, awestruck. Perhaps he didn't look so foolish after all, Sedge thought, brightening a little.

'Is it time then?' Silken said. She was holding herself very still and stiff, as though scared her wreath would fall off. Her evident nervousness made Sedge feel better. He took her paw.

'Nearly. Come on.'

The little group moved slowly through the trees to the water's edge, where the holt had begun to gather. The flood was glowing silver now in the light of the great full moon – which hung so low that Silken felt she could touch it if she only reached a little higher. Their wreaths of white flowers drew the light, so that next to her Sedge seemed to be wearing a glowing crown. She tightened her paw in his, and he nodded seriously at her. Together, they padded through the shallow skin of water, and the otters around them shuffled and splashed as they made an arc facing out towards the river, the broken holt at their backs.

Silken shivered as the water lapped around their paws and tails. Surely it hadn't been this cold earlier on?

The otters began to whisper and chant together, and the eerie coldness wove up Silken's spine and held her. She knew these words – they were ones the holt had been singing to the river for many otter lifetimes. How could she have forgotten?

The words sang inside her, and Silken sang with the holt, lifting her paws out to the water and reaching for Lady River. Beside her she felt Sedge do the same. Silken met his eyes, and saw that they were glittering with fear and excitement.

She could see that he was asking, *Do you feel it too?* and she widened her eyes in answer. Silken glanced round at Thorn, standing next to them with Teasel on her other side, both with eyes closed and paws outstretched.

Silken had been shocked when she first saw her mother. In that strange rush of memory that had returned after she'd rescued Sedge, Thorn had been tall and strong, bright-eyed and gleeful. Silken remembered her leaping around in the shallow water as she and Teasel taught them to swim. She had been busy, sometimes even weighed down by the cares of the holt, but she had been full of life. When they met in the floodwater, her mother had seemed frail and old. When had she aged so? When Silken disappeared, or when Sedge did?

Now, wading into the waters together, there was something of that past energy in her mother's gaze. She was no longer stooped – she stood straight and strong, crowned with white meadowsweet and tiny glowing waterlilies. The shining crown made her eyes look huge and dark, and the silver frost over her fur glittered.

The otters' song rose around Thorn as she stepped

forward, lifting her paws out towards the rushing river. Sedge had said that their mother had given up singing, except for the strange, stale ceremonies. She hadn't been able to sing her love to the river, not after that same river had stolen away her cub.

She thought the river had stolen me, Silken thought, as the current tugged at her paws, and the silty river bottom swirled under them. *But now that the river has given me back – we can sing together. If I stay . . .*

Cautiously, Silken reached out one paw to her mother, near but not quite touching, so she could dart it back again if this was wrong. But Thorn turned her head and snatched at her daughter, twining their paws together. Her eyes were dancing. She squeezed Silken's paw tightly in her own, nodding towards the water, and Silken gasped a breath, and sang.

> *River, won't you feed us,*
> *Each and every day,*
> *River, won't you help us,*
> *Safe by your waters stay.*

Sedge was singing too, still gripping her paw on the other side, and Silken could feel the otters of the holt gathered behind the three of them. The swell of their voices added to her song, and the song was *in* the water, all around them.

> *River, still we need you,*
> *Each and every day,*
> *River, now we fear you,*
> *Don't sweep our homes away.*

> *River, please protect us,*
> *Each and every day,*
> *River, wrap around us,*
> *Care for every stray.*

The otters dropped their voices then, so that Thorn could sing the last verse alone.

> *River, let me thank you,*
> *You brought them back to me.*
> *River, now I hear you,*
> *Your true love I see.*

Willow and Marigold were standing in front of them now with rough baskets of willow twigs, all piled up with flowers. The cubs cast the petals across the water and Silken saw them swirl and circle around her and Sedge and Thorn. *Was the river doing that?* Silken wondered, holding her breath. Or were the flowers only caught in an eddy, a strange knot of water? She wanted so much to believe the river was there with them, wrapping the three of them in a cool embrace. Perhaps she was only wishing.

From the edge of the flood came a hushed and joyful whispering, as the watching otters pointed out the petals to each other, the way the water was seeping slowly through their dark fur, stippling them with white petal stars.

'Go,' Thorn murmured to Sedge and Silken. 'Out into the true river. This is your time.'

'Come with us,' Sedge pleaded, and Silken reached out to her mother, but Thorn stepped back, her whiskers quivering. 'Tell her for me,' she said, resting her head against Teasel's shoulder.

Together, Sedge and Silken plunged forward into the deeper water of the main channel, the true heart of the river. They could hear the otters of the holt singing behind them, the voices dancing over the water. The young otters dived below the surface, clouds of moonlight-silver bubbles rising from their fur, and sank into the river's embrace.

She was there, with them. A white otter darting and turning and swirling in delight. Her shining fur brushed

223

theirs as they swam and dived, glorying in the water. They reached out to press their paws to her coat as she swooped by, and even those brief brushes against her dazzling fur filled them with a deep, unexplainable happiness.

You came back to me, a voice murmured in the water. *My otters.*

We never went away, Sedge protested. *We were here all the time. You left us!* Then he twisted, blinking and looking around as he tried to understand where his voice was coming from.

How could I leave, when this is my river? the voice said, and the water around them seemed full of laughter. *No matter now.*

Why are you an otter? Silken burst out, and Sedge swam closer, his eyes narrowed in confusion. The white otter stalled in the water, gazing at Silken with interest.

What are you, little sister? Tell me.

An otter – I think. Silken's water-voice was small.

You are an otter! Sedge beat the water with his paws. *How many times do we have to tell you?*

It isn't something that can be told, the white otter murmured. She swam closer, coiling tightly around the two of them, and nuzzling gently at Silken. *But your brother is right. You are an otter, and so am I. We are both creatures of the water, and of the bank. Otters live the river, the way I do. When you swim, you belong to the water. But my river isn't only water, you must see that. I am the silt and the stones and the roots of trees. The fish, all the creatures who lean down to drink. The beavers.* She laid her paw gently against Silken's muzzle. *You are not a beaver, little sister, but you know the lodge, and their way. Now you are learning to be an otter again. You must weave both lives together.*

She swirled in the water, reappearing next to Sedge. *You have learned too, dear one.* She chuckled again, a rich sound of water pattering over stones. *Dearly beloved of the river. You never know how much you love something until you leave it. You saved your sister, but you could only do that by taking another life. That should never grow easy.* Her voice grew stronger as she addressed them both. *Rebuild your holt, my otters. My waters will run gently, lapping past your door.*

The white otter shimmered, and then seemed to melt away into the water, water that wrapped lovingly around Silken and Sedge. The river lifted them both back to the murmuring band of otters, trembling and dazed. Their flower crowns were gone, but each of them wore a circlet of glittering water drops.

The gathered otters stared at them silently, and then Silken shook herself, and Sedge sneezed.

The spell of silence whispered away, and Thorn reached out to press them tightly against her. 'We saw,' she said. 'We saw the white otter. Lady River.'

'Look! Look at the water!' Soft, wondering voices rose around Sedge and Silken as the otters watched the floodwater begin to seep away. A scent of dark, rich mud rose around them, and they lifted their paws out of the sticky mass, laughing. Then they turned toward the great willow tree, looking anxiously at their holt.

Water was draining slowly out of the tunnels, and a small, scarlet-finned fish flapped gasping against a tree root. Tormentil batted at it with a paw, scooping it back into the river, and then blinked, as though she didn't quite know what she had done.

'She told us to rebuild,' Sedge began to say, and then he broke off, nudging Silken with his shoulder. 'Look. Over there, on the bank. Someone was watching the ceremony.'

Silken looked over, and her breath caught. The draining of the water had stranded someone in the reeds, a dark shape, bunchy and strong. He stood stone-still, but two deep-set eyes glittered in the moonlight.

She raised her paw hesitantly, and the figure nodded back.

He waited for a moment, eyeing the watching crowd of otters, and then the Master Beaver slipped into the water, and began to paddle downstream, taking the news back to the lodge.

'Sing for us, Silken,' the two smallest otters begged, popping up beside her in the kitchen and pulling on her paws.

Silken glanced round at her mother, who was scooping layers of dirt and sticks out of the corners. Two days after their return, the holt was still full of mud and mess, but Silken was starting to see that it could be a home. Maybe even a home for her.

'Sing a *new* song,' Marigold insisted, and Lady Thorn straightened up, easing her spine, and nodded. Sedge and the other young otters stopped sweeping and perched on the massive wooden table to listen. Bramble the cook stopped counting jars of preserves, and leaned against the table too. Silken's whiskers trembled a little. She wasn't used to singing to such an eager audience, and it still felt strange.

'I made this song for someone we met on our journey,' she explained, while she waited for Marigold and Willow to stop squirming and settle. They were squashed up next to her now, practically sitting on her tail. 'He's a swan, an old swan who's lived on the Greenriver for a long time. This is his song.'

She coughed a little, and then closed her eyes so as not to see them all watching her.

When the mist lies on the river,
I see you.
Or when the dawn breaks cold and grey.

When the sun shines on the water,
Then I see you.
And when the wind sighs in the trees.

When the shadows grow at evening,
It's then I see you.
Whenever night is drawing in.

When a swan flies down the river,
I see not them, but only you.
And my heart tears deep inside.

Silken kept her eyes closed when she'd finished singing. She was thinking of Vane, and his hoarse voice as she spoke of his mate.

'What happened to him?' Marigold whispered. 'The old swan?'

'He lost his mate in the flood,' Sedge told her, when Silken didn't speak. 'Then he found Silken and took her to be cared for at the beavers' lodge, that same day. He asked us to remember her.'

'Her name was Quill,' Silken said quietly.

'I would like it, if that song was about me,' Willow said, nuzzling the top of her head under Silken's chin. 'Everyone will hear it, up and down the river, and they'll be so sad. But then afterwards they'll be glad they listened.'

Silken lifted her head at last to look at Sedge, and then at her mother. Both of them were gazing back at her, their eyes dark and proud.

She was Silken Greenriver.

She was an otter who had come home.

Letters, Carried Up and Down the River

Honoured Master Grey,

The swan Vane has agreed to carry this message to you. We thank you for the care of our child Elderberry, known to you, and now to us, as Silken. She has told us much about her life among your people. We would wish to know more about the Stronghold and its ways, and we hope that you would be glad to hear news of your adopted child.

We are all creatures of the river, however differently we spend our days around her waters.

Our good wishes for your lodge, and your safe rebuilding.

Thorn, Lady of Greenriver Holt

Dear Lady Thorn,

Thank you, for your message, and for the gift of
your child.

    We did not understand how much she was to us
until we lost her.

    When our lodge is safe and whole once more,
messengers from the Stronghold will come upriver. We
long to see our daughter again.

Grey, Master Builder of the Stronghold

Acknowledgements

Thank you so much to everyone who has helped this book on its way.

To Ruth Alltimes for that first otter chat in the café with the brilliant river view at Hachette.

To Lena McCauley for your wonderful insights into the story – I had a medium-sized panic at the first editorial email, but you were right about it all!

To Genevieve Herr, for removing all the whispering, and making me think carefully about every word.

To Zanna Goldhawk, for the beautiful cover and clever, enchanting illustrations – so exciting to see my otters!

To Lynne Manning, for making the whole book look so wonderful.

To Julia Churchill, for fabulous phone calls and cat photos and making me believe this book would work, as well as enormous amounts of plot inspiration. Really, really could not have done this without you!

To Stephanie Burgis, for wonderful words of encouragement – it made such a difference!

To my family, Jon, Ash, Robin and Will, for putting up with me dragging you to look at rivers – and for reading it first.